~NOTHING~

SAVING MAGIC
BOOK ONE

JENNIFER REDMILE

Cover Designer: Jennifer Redmile

CHAPTER ONE

Molly

*L*aughter echoed off the walls, the distorted faces and hateful words flooding my mind as I ran. The faces of my tormentors were somehow distorted, like the reflections in the mirrors at a carnival. And even though I kept running, the door to the outside world and the freedom it represented didn't seem to be getting any closer.

How was that even possible? It felt like I'd been running forever.

Leg muscles screaming in protest, I looked for another way out. I knew I couldn't stop. Not until I'd escaped the voices. Relief flooded through me when a door appeared up ahead to my left. But the relief quickly evaporated when four people spilled out to stand in front of me, their faces twisted with hate.

Damnit, why couldn't they just leave me alone?

I stopped—well, it was either that or barrel into them—contemplating running back the way I'd come. Which is when I realised the girl's hate-filled eyes were staring not at me but at something, or rather someone, beside me.

"Oooh... where'd you get your new toy, Molly? You growing your own Nothing playmates now?"

The rest of the group sniggered, and I desperately wanted to shove them out of my way.

"Why the hell can't you just leave me alone?" I whispered, my voice hoarse from the burning rage threatening to escape.

The girl's eyes had started to glow with her own not-quite-suppressed rage. "How dare you speak to me. You know that Nothings should be seen and not heard! Get outta my face before I do something that'll make you regret ever being born."

She suddenly looked like a volcano ready to erupt. But when her lips started moving, her hands clenching into fists, I could only stare at her in horror.

Oh. My. God. The girl had obviously lost her mind. Surely she wasn't stupid enough to consider using her magic to harm another person. It was illegal! But even as I held up a hand, shaking my head and looking into her crazed eyes, I knew it was too late to make her see reason. The volcano had already erupted.

An evil grin spread across her face as she flicked her wrist towards me. Closing my eyes, I braced for the impact, knowing there was nothing I could do to defend myself.

Pain lanced through my body as the power hit me in the chest, lifting me off my feet and sending me flying through the air. I hit the wall with a resounding crunch, feeling my bones shatter from the impact... and I woke up.

I sat up in bed, shaking and soaked with sweat. Sucking in huge gulps of air, I pondered the new twist in my usually repetitive nightmare. *There was someone else there with me... and they were a Nothing too.*

CHAPTER TWO

Molly

"*M*olly! Hurry up! You're gonna be late for school… *again*."

Groaning, I pulled the pillow over my head as Mum's voice drifted up from the kitchen. Like I cared if I was late. School was just another name for *Hades* as far as I was concerned. The thought of burning for all of eternity didn't sound so bad when compared to being bullied by a bunch of sadistic teenagers.

"*Now, Molly!*" Damnit. Mum's voice had that *edge* to it. You know, the one where they sound like they're being patient, but their head is actually ready to explode. Then I was gagging as the mental image of Mum's head literally exploding grossed me out. *Seriously? Why did I have to be born with a warped brain on top of everything else?*

"Yeah, I'm coming," I called, throwing the blankets back and dragging my butt out of bed. "Just getting dressed." Because imagining exploding heads aside, my mum in a cranky mood was a whole other world of bad.

"Five minutes…"

Tossing the pillow across the room, I sat up and pushed my unruly bed hair back from my face. Sometimes, my life felt like a version of that movie, *Groundhog Day*, except maybe worse. I mean, at least some of what happened in *his* day was good.

Yeah, whatever. Pulling on the jeans and t-shirt I'd left out the previous night, I dragged a brush through my hair and pulled it into a ponytail. I thought about applying some makeup just for a second, then scoffed at the ridiculous thought. Why bother? Staring into the mirror at the plain, brown-haired, brown-eyed seventeen-year-old girl looking back at me, I wished for the gazillionth time I could be normal.

Never. Going. To. Happen.

Grabbing my school bag and throwing it over my shoulder, I ran down the stairs, congratulating myself for only taking two minutes to get ready. *Wow, miracles really did happen.* Maybe today wouldn't be as bad as—

I reached the kitchen door and froze, the good start to the day gurgling as it slipped down the drain. *Unbelievable.* My stomach turned as I watched Mum's magic preparing breakfast. The coffee pot and carton of milk floated through the air towards the kitchen table, the butter knife efficiently buttering the toast while the spatula lifted the eggs from the pan and slipped them onto the waiting plates.

Then I caught sight of Mum looking up from doing her makeup in the mirror. Her face held both surprise at my quick appearance and an apologetic wince. "Sorry honey, I have an early meeting and needed some help with breakfast. I'm sure you can cope just this once?"

Normally, I could have. But with the dream still so fresh in my mind, the last thing I needed today was to have my status as a genetic reject thrown in my face. Okay, so I knew Mum would be devastated if she'd known I'd react this way. But my *I-don't-give-a-shit-ometer* levels were at an all-time low right then.

"Ummm… actually, I'm not hungry." I backed out of the room, managing a weak smile as the anger, envy, and shame battled for supremacy. "I'll see you tonight…"

Quickly turning away from the magical display, I raced for the front door before she could say anything. I knew it was stupid, but sometimes, just seeing magic being used so casually made my eyes burn. By the time I climbed into my car, backed out of the driveway and headed down the road towards school, the tears were streaming down my face. Damn it! I hated crying almost as much as I hated school.

Why me? Why did I have to be born a freak? Yep, and now the self-pity had kicked in too. Talk about the world going to *hell in a hand-basket*. Today was rapidly climbing the ladder in my ridiculously long list of *days I should have stayed in bed*. And I still wasn't even at school yet!

Magic, or the lack thereof, had been the bane of my existence since my thirteenth birthday. That was the day I'd been told I was a Nothing! Yep, that's the name given to those of us *freaks* unlucky enough to be born without access to any form of magic whatsoever. My chest tightened at the memory of the doctor telling Mum that although the condition had been almost eradicated in today's society, a *throwback* to our magic-less ancestors now and then was unavoidable.

And just like that, my life had changed irrevocably. Prior to that day, I'd been looking forward to starting High School all year. But that was *before* everyone found out what I was. It was like I'd contracted some highly contagious disease. Girls I'd thought friends either avoided me or huddled together, snickering and pointing when I passed by. I'd become a pariah.

Pulling over to the side of the road, I pried my white-knuckled hands from the steering wheel. Damnit, I *refused* to arrive at school with puffy red eyes. It would only give the Magics even more ammu-nition. I leaned my head against the steering wheel, inhaling and exhaling slowly until my heart rate returned to normal.

I needed to pull myself together. So what if Mum had used her magic in front of me? It's not like I didn't know everyone else in my family had magic. It's just that they usually tried not to use it when I was around. If only I'd taken longer getting ready for school. I'd never have even known she'd used magic to prepare breakfast!

Okay, enough. Self-pity was a stupid waste of time and energy. I glanced at my watch and realised how late I was... again. Sucking in a deep breath and straightening my shoulders, I pulled away from the kerb and headed toward school. Oh well, at least being this late meant everyone would be in class already. The *walk of shame* would be averted one more time. A small win on just another day in the hell that was my life. *Yay me...*

"LATE AGAIN, MOLLY." Mrs Perch, the school office lady, peered at me over her horn-rimmed glasses. Damn the woman. Over the years, she'd perfected the ability to make me feel more like a cockroach than a human being. I quickly looked down at the floor to hide my smile as another one of those ridiculous thoughts popped into my head.

Does that mean that cockroaches are above or below Nothings in the grand scheme of things? Not that it was important, but still...

I waited for her to blink my details onto a late note, biting my tongue to stop myself from responding to the words of disapproval she muttered under her breath. She knew they were loud enough for me to hear and was now literally baiting the cockroach. But I knew the consequences of responding to her taunts from experience and would not fall for that trick *ever* again. Finally, she cleared her throat to get my attention, and as I looked up, she thrust the note under my nose.

"Thanks," I muttered, refusing to make eye contact with the condescending cow as I took the note and turned towards my classroom. Gritting my teeth, I walked down the empty corridor, hating myself for the relief I felt when no one was around.

Seriously, when had I become so pathetic? I'd spent the last four years building a shell around myself, determined not to give them the satisfaction of knowing how much their cruel words hurt me. Lifting my chin, I walked past the classroom labelled *Telekinetics 101*, ignoring the urge to duck below the small viewing window, and continued towards the *Special Education* room.

Yep, that's what they called the education delivered to the ever-decreasing number of Nothings. Out of the hundred kids in my final year of school, there were only twelve Nothings, which was less than half the number of freaks in the previous year. Apparently, the condition was indeed becoming less prevalent.

Sucking in a deep breath, I opened the door to my classroom and stepped inside. *It's just another day... nothing more, nothing less.*

"Aah, Ms Chambers. I'm so pleased you decided to grace us with your presence." Mr. Krock's voice dripped with sarcasm, his beady eyes taking in my dishevelled appearance. His eyebrows lifted, and I got that weird tingling sensation telling me Krock was using magic. Probably scanning my mind for the details of my morning's drama. I couldn't help wondering how much he saw.

"Hmmm," he said, a thoughtful look on his face as he took the late note. "Please sit down and take out your history book."

Moving towards my seat in the third row, I tried to ignore the stares of my classmates. *What? Did I grow a second head overnight or something?* Determined to appear unaffected, I slipped into my seat and bent down to pull my book out of my bag. Okay, so I was even a freak to the other Nothings. *Whatever.*

Startled by a tug on my ponytail, I turned to find Mark Johns, the biggest jerk in the class, leering at me. The guy seriously gave me the creeps.

"Hey, Molly Mouse. Looking grumpy as usual. Need a hug?"

"Bite me," I growled, turning back to the front of the classroom. Despite my constant rejection, Mark had spent the first year of high school trying to get me to go out with him. When he'd finally realised he didn't have a hope in hell, he'd turned into an even bigger pain in the butt.

A deep, throaty chuckle emerged from the previously vacant seat beside Mark. I slowly turned back around to find a perfect stranger sitting in said seat, grinning from ear to ear. And believe me, the guy was about as close to *perfect* as humanly possible. His scruffy, sandy blonde hair hung over eyes as blue as the ocean on a summer's day. My face burned as those sparkling blue eyes met mine. *Wow. Where had he come from?*

I swivelled back towards the front at the sound of Mr. Krock clearing his throat. *Oh great, like I wasn't in enough trouble already.*

"So, as I was saying when Ms Chambers arrived, I'd like to introduce our new class member. Tray has just moved here from Sydney. Perhaps you'd like to tell us a bit about yourself, Mr. Harper?"

At the sound of Tray's chair being pushed back, I gave in to the urge to turn back around and stare at his perfect features. He stood and folded his arms, a stance that managed to accentuate his bulging biceps. Not that I noticed, of course.

Tray's eyes twinkled with mischief as they landed on me. "Not much to tell, really. We had to move here 'cos of my dad's work commitments. So here I am living in beautiful, downtown… Medulla."

The name of our small town came out sounding like a death toll. I suppose for someone who'd lived in

Sydney, that's what moving here would feel like. He obviously wasn't happy about the move. Not that I blamed him. Medulla was far from a thriving metropolis. In fact, it was the epitome of a boring hole, especially for a Nothing.

Mr. Krock opened his mouth as if to ask Tray something else, obviously rethinking his decision at the closed look on Tray's face as he hastily sat back down.

"Right… well, welcome to Medulla." Clearing his throat, Mr Krock turned his attention to the rest of the class. "So, for the benefit of Mr Harper, who can summarise what we learned in yesterday's history lesson? I believe we were up to the election of the First Mage Council?"

As if on cue, Stacey Hollice's hand shot into the air. Stacey was the class princess—*well, in her opinion anyway*—and she was obviously trying to impress the hot new guy with her knowledge. I couldn't resist sneaking a glance at Tray's reaction out of the corner of my eye. The obvious lack of interest on Tray's face at both Stacey *and* her regurgitation of yesterday's lesson had me covering my mouth to hide a smile.

Huh! Suck rocks, Stacey. Of course, he caught me looking at him, the sparkle flashing back into his eyes when he saw the smile I was trying to hide.

By the time the bell rang for recess, I was a flustered mess. My reaction to the new guy in the class was just plain weird. I'd never been so affected by another person's presence. *Maybe I was coming down with something?*

Grabbing my bag, I practically ran to the door, needing to get outside so I could start breathing normally again. *Get a grip, Molly... he is just a guy, for magic's sake.*

I pushed the doors to the outside area open, hurrying to my usual spot under a tree near the back fence. When I finally reached it, I dropped to the ground and breathed a sigh of relief. Okay, I had a whole fifteen minutes to pull myself together. I had no idea why I was reacting this way to some guy. It wasn't like I'd ever met one that was worth even talking to, no matter how good-looking they were.

"There you are. I was just about to give up looking for you," a deep voice said from the other side of the tree. I recognised it as Tray's immediately.

Oh great, did he think I'd been hiding or something? "Yeah, sorry about that. I'm not used to anyone looking for me, to be honest," I said, blushing profusely.

"Well, more fool them. Do you mind if I join you? I don't exactly have people falling over themselves to sit with me, either."

I couldn't help smiling at that. If he'd bothered to look around, just about every girl in the playground would have killed to have him sit with them. "Well, in that case, feel free to hide… oops, I mean, *sit* with me."

We both smiled at my weak attempt at humour and then he settled down beside me.

An awkward silence hung in the air as if neither of us knew what to say. I was desperately trying to think of something witty when he finally spoke.

"Sooo… do I really have to call you Miss Chambers?" He grinned, and I found myself grinning right back.

"It's Molly…"

"Molly… yep, it suits you."

"Well, I'm glad you think so. Cos I have no intention of changing it."

Tray threw back his head and laughed. "Go you. It's nice to find another Nothing whose status hasn't turned them into a spineless wuss. I'd almost given up hope."

A thrill of pleasure ran through me at his compliment. Was he saying he liked me? "Surely you've met lots of other Nothings who refuse to be doormats? I mean, magic isn't everything."

"Yeah, right. Try telling that to those who have it!" he scoffed, his fists clenching.

"Sorry. Sounds like I hit a sore spot."

Tray blew out a breath, unclenched his fists, and ran his hands through his hair. "No… *I'm* sorry. Great first impression. You must think I'm a total whack job."

Tilting my head, I looked into his gorgeous blue eyes. *Maybe I did, but at least he was a good to look at whack job.* "Hey, it's cool. We all have our own personal demons to live with. I don't think there's a Nothing on earth that's happy with their lot in life. It sucks... but what can you do?"

Holding my gaze, Tray gave me a sad smile and nodded. Wow. I'd never had this kind of conversation with *anyone*, preferring to keep my feelings about not having magic to myself. It was comforting to know I wasn't the only person in the world who felt like this.

Since being snubbed by my friends when they'd discovered I was a Nothing, I'd been loath to encourage friendships, even with others like me. I mean... what was the point? I had enough people in my world who had the power to hurt me. Why invite more? But then, maybe Tray would turn out to be worth the risk.

The sound of the end-of-recess bell pulled me from my thoughts, my face warming when I realised I'd been staring at Tray the whole time. *Oh God... I must look like some love-struck moron.* But Tray just smiled, jumped to his feet, and held out a hand to help me up. His hand closed around mine, and I could feel the blush spreading over my skin. *Seriously? For magic's sake, Molly. Get a grip.*

Tray just smiled as he let go of my hand. He didn't even mention the embarrassing state of my skin, and for that alone my opinion of him rose another notch. We walked back to the classroom together, and I was surprised by how comfortable I felt in Tray's company.

CHAPTER THREE

Tray

*O**kay, so maybe moving to Medulla might not be so bad after all.* Walking back to class beside Molly actually felt normal. I hadn't realised just how much I'd missed having a feminine presence in my life, with Mum and Emily no longer living with us. I mean, Dad was great, but it just wasn't the same. It would be so cool if Molly and I became friends.

What surprised me was how much I wanted to impress her, which was weird because it wasn't like I was attracted to her. But something about Molly's thick, unruly brown hair and soulful chocolate-brown eyes made me want to scoop her up and protect her from all that was wrong in this world. Which, when you were a Nothing, was a helluva lot.

We reached the doorway to the classroom, and

Molly threw me a shy smile as she moved to her seat. I returned the smile and caught Mark, the dork who sat next to me, raising an eyebrow as I slipped into my seat. He leaned over and whispered overly loud. "Don't waste your time with that one. She's the ice queen of Medulla."

Molly stiffened in her seat, and I wanted to punch the guy in the head. Instead, I said in the same overly loud whisper. "Sounds like sour grapes to me. Maybe she's just not into douchebags."

Ignoring his scowl, I noticed Molly's shoulders shaking with laughter. *Damn, that felt good.* Seriously, something about being around this girl made the world feel not quite so bleak. Having to leave all my friends in Sydney behind had been painful, and it had been a long time since I'd felt this close to being happy. Not surprising, really, considering how much my life had turned to shit in the last couple of months.

As if being born a Nothing wasn't punishment enough, the universe just couldn't help twisting the knife and exposing me as an even bigger freak. And now, here I was in the middle of Nowheresville with Dad while Mum and Emmy had to stay behind in Sydney. That was the part that hurt the most. Our family had been torn apart because of me.

So much for the good mood I'd been in. I tried to focus on what the teacher was saying, but my eyes were drawn to Molly constantly. I wondered if she was thinking about me.

Why would she Dufus? She probably thinks you're just some moody nutjob.

I closed my eyes and tried to remember how to be the slightly more well-adjusted Nothing I used to be. Before that day when I'd walked into the basement, and my world had imploded. I'd had friends and had accepted my lot in life as a Nothing. Now, I just needed to get back to that place and stop being angry about things I couldn't change. Who knew? Maybe having a friend like Molly could help me get back to that place. Well, it was worth a try…

Molly

LUNCH WAS ALMOST over when I looked up from my book to see Tray heading toward me. My heart skipped a beat as he gave me a sheepish smile, shuffling his feet as he leaned against the tree beside me.

"Bloody paperwork," he muttered.

"Sorry?" *Great, he was in a bad mood again.*

"I just spent the whole of lunch in the office filling out paperwork."

My stomach felt as if a swarm of butterflies had invaded it. *So, he hadn't been avoiding me. He'd just been busy.* "Oh well, it's not like you missed much." I cringed at the sound of my high-pitched, breathy voice. *Seriously, Molly, enough.*

Tray sighed and ran his hand through his hair. "It's just… I enjoyed our chat at recess and was looking forward to—"

I wanted to scream as the end-of-lunch bell rang, cutting off what he'd been about to say. *Damnit, couldn't anything in my life go right, just for once?* Stuffing my book into my bag, I scrambled to my feet, avoiding his eyes as I remembered the embarrassing 'hand touching' thing from earlier. No way I was going *there* again.

Tray pushed away from the tree and fell into step beside me. "So… maybe we could… ummm… do lunch together tomorrow?"

O.M.G. The damn butterflies had morphed into a marauding army of wasps. *Why would someone like Tray be interested in me? Oh wait, he didn't know anyone else. Maybe he was hoping I'd introduce him around. Although surely he'd noticed I wasn't exactly the society belle of Nothings.*

I shrugged, trying to pull off what I hoped looked like an *it's-no-big-deal-for-a-hot-guy-to-want-to-have-lunch-with-me* look as I met his gorgeous blue eyes. "Sure… if you want."

Magic's balls, looking at him was a huge mistake. I stumbled—*yes, I actually tripped over my own feet*—and he grabbed my arm to stop me from falling. Heat rushed to my face yet again. Seriously? Tray would start to think I had some kind of skin disorder.

"You okay?" he asked.

"Yeah, thanks… must have stepped in a hole or something," I mumbled, wishing a really *big* hole would open up beneath my feet so I could disappear into it.

His hand finally left my arm, and he stuffed it in his pocket. *What the hell was going on with me? I'd never acted like this before in my life. In fact, it had always made me sick to watch girls who acted like this around guys.*

Reaching the classroom, we shared an awkward smile before going to our desks. I groaned as I plopped into my chair. This was all too hard. I needed this day to be over so I could go home and bury my head in my pillow.

Surprisingly, the afternoon lesson flew, and the relief of the day being over *almost* overrode the usual sick feeling in the pit of my stomach at the sound of the final bell. It was time for another *walk of shame*, except this time, the corridors wouldn't be empty. Taunting the Nothings was a game the Magics never seemed to grow tired of. Picking up my bag, I headed for the door, squaring my shoulders and preparing for the onslaught. *Maybe today wouldn't be so…*

Yeah, right; who was I trying to kid? It would be a nightmare… as always.

I'd just started to walk toward the exit when a familiar, deep voice called out from behind me.

"Hey, Molly… wait up." I turned to find Tray

hurrying to catch up to me. "Can I walk you to your car? I assume this school is like all the others I've been to… and the usual bullies will be waiting?"

"Yeah, but I can handle it. Same crap, different day," I said with a shrug.

Tray chuckled and fell in beside me. "Cool. I'll try not to get in your way then."

We walked in silence, my heart hammering in my chest as I anticipated today's torture. We were almost halfway to the exit door when a group of kids stepped out of a classroom in front of us. The hairs on the back of my neck stood up. *Shit on a stick... this was my dream coming to life.* Except that I recognised the faces of the four people standing in front of me. Mandy Sykes, my best friend up until my thirteenth birthday, was in the group. For the last four years, she'd made it her personal goal to punish me for "turning into a Nothing". *Like I had a choice!*

Mandy's eyes widened as she took in Tray's perfection, narrowing as they moved to me. "Oooh… the Nothingness is growing. Where'd you get your new toy, *Molly*? You growing your own playmates now?"

The rest of the group sniggered, and my blood started to boil. I'd learned years ago not to respond to the taunts. It only ever made things worse. But for the first time in a long time, they got to me. Maybe it was having Tray there to witness my humiliation, but something seemed to burst inside me, and I just couldn't let it go any more. Instead of the whispered plea from my dream, I lifted my chin and glared at my nemesis.

"Seriously, Mandy? Don't you ever get sick of tormenting people? You really need to get a life."

The look of shock on her face almost made me laugh. I think it was the fact that I'd actually stood up to her, rather than the words I'd spoken, that caused her mouth to start flapping like a guppy. Just for a second, I thought I might have actually rendered her speechless. Miracles really *did* happen.

But then she rallied, "How *dare* you speak to me. Don't you know that Nothing should be seen and not heard? Get outta my face before I do something that'll make you wish you'd never been born."

I felt the heat of Tray's hand on the small of my back as Mandy's face twisted with rage. The dream was back on replay. Yep, this was the part where she looked like a volcano ready to blow. I stared at her in fascination as her lips started to move and her hands clenched into fists. *Wait... no way this could be happening.* This wasn't a dream—it was real life. And Mandy was planning to use her magic against me? I took a step back, aware of Tray's arm slipping around my waist. Okay, I didn't remember *that* from the dream.

An evil grin spread across Mandy's face as she flicked her wrist towards me. I felt Tray try to pull me out of the path of the magic, but it was too late. I closed my eyes and braced myself for the impact. But instead of the expected thrust of power hitting me in the chest, like in the dream, I got a tingling sensation like when Krock was reading my mind. *Seriously? She'd sent me the tingles? What was with that?*

When I opened my eyes, the group stood in front of me, white-faced and open-mouthed. Mandy took a step back as if suddenly afraid of me. *What the hell was going on?*

Tray's hand slipped from my waist, and he grabbed my hand. "We need to get out of here... *now!*" he whispered in my ear, and the next thing I knew, he was pulling me down the corridor towards the exit sign. Tray wore the closed look I was already getting used to. I looked back as we reached the doors. No one in the group of bullies had moved or said a word.

As soon as the doors closed behind us, I pulled my hand out of Tray's and planted my feet, hands on hips. "Okay... enough. What the hell just happened? Why does everyone look so... shell-shocked?"

Tray frowned down at me. "Do you really not know what just happened?"

"Seriously. If I knew, why would I bother to ask?"

Tray's eyes widened, a smile lifting the corner of his mouth. "Wow... you seriously have no idea. Come on, let's get to your car, and we can talk. Which car is yours?"

He reached for my hand again, but I stamped my foot, feeling like a four-year-old. "Listen. I'm not going anywhere until I know what's going on."

Tray ran his hand through his hair and took a deep

breath. "Okay. I recognised that spell Mandy was chanting, and there's no way you should have been still standing there after she cast it. So, either she stuffed up, which I very much doubt, or… you're immune to magic."

Say what? My jaw dropped as I tried to digest what he'd just said. "So, the spell wasn't just supposed to make me tingle all over?"

Tray laughed. "Nope, you should have been airborne and ended up sprawled on the floor or splattered against a wall at the other end of the corridor."

Just like in my dream. "But… this is insane. There's no such thing as being *immune* to magic. So how—?"

"Honestly? I have no idea. But I don't think hanging around to find out what happens next is the best idea."

My brain finally kicked back into gear. There *had* to be a simple explanation for what happened. I just needed time to think. "Okay. Blue Micra at the far end of the parking lot on the left."

Warmth spread over me at the feel of Tray's hand once again pressed against my lower back. Why was he being so considerate to someone he'd only just met? And where on earth had he come up with the idea that I was immune to magic? But then, why *hadn't* the magic worked on me? It had always worked in my dream. Wait. Maybe I was still asleep, and this whole day had been a dream? *Damnit, I hope not. I so want Tray to be real.*

I pinched myself and smiled. *Yep, definitely awake.*

Okay, so it must have had something to do with Mandy's spell going wrong. But whatever had happened, there would be *a lot* of questions asked. I still couldn't believe Mandy would even *think* of using her magic against another person.

We reached the car, and Tray turned me to face him. "You need to go straight home. Maybe Mandy and her group of goons will have enough sense not to report the incident. Hopefully, the fear of how much trouble she'd be in for trying to use her magic on you will stop her from telling anyone what happened."

A weird sense of numbness crept through my body as the reality of the situation hit me. Whatever happened, some serious shit had gone down in that hallway. I nodded and realised my hands were shaking when I started to fumble through my bag for my keys. Tray was right about one thing. I needed to get home.

He grabbed my shaking hand with one of his, using the other to lift my chin to look at him. "Hey… are you okay?"

I focused on his eyes, sucked in a deep breath, and tried to pull myself together. "Y…yep. I'm f…fine." I said, knowing I sounded far from it.

"Look, I'm probably blowing the whole thing out of proportion. But maybe don't mention what happened to anyone, just in case. We can talk about it tomorrow if you want. Okay?"

"Sure." Seemingly satisfied, he let my hand go, and I finally located my elusive keys. But my damn hands were still shaking so badly I couldn't seem to get the key in the door, and the damned tears were welling for the second time that day.

Tray reached for the keys, and I handed them over, disgusted with myself for acting like such a feeble idiot. Without a word, he opened the door and put the key into the ignition. "You sure you're okay to drive? 'Cos I can always…"

"No. I'm fine. Th…thanks, I'll see you tomorrow." He looked at me like he wanted to say more, then shook his head, stepping aside so I could climb into the car. I forced a smile onto my face—which probably looked more like a grimace— started the engine and pulled out of the parking spot, giving him a quick wave as I drove away. That was about as normal as it was going to get after the day I'd had.

I looked back in the rear-view mirror and saw Tray standing where I'd left him, his arms folded and a worried frown on his face. I had a really bad feeling things were going to get a helluva lot worse before they got better.

CHAPTER FOUR

Tray

By the time I got home, my head was pounding, and my stomach churned with nausea. The same question had been playing on repeat the whole way home. *Could Molly really be an Immune?*

"Dad? You home?"

"Hey, Tray. I'm in the kitchen. Come tell me all about your first day at the new school."

Groaning, I threw my bag down in the hallway and walked into the kitchen. I couldn't decide whether I wanted to throw up or laugh hysterically. After all Dad had been through, this was the last thing he needed to hear.

His smile vanished the minute he set eyes on me. "Okay… what happened?"

I flopped down onto a stool at the breakfast bar and

buried my face in my hands. "Shit Dad. I wish I knew. I mean, I know it sounds ridiculous, but do you think it's possible there might be another Immune at my new school?"

All the blood seemed to drain from Dad's face. "What the hell? Why would you even ask that?"

I lifted my head and saw the old familiar panic back in his eyes. Shit… I hated knowing I was the cause of that. This nightmare just kept getting worse.

"Tray. Tell me what happened."

I looked down at my clenched fists on the breakfast bar and shared what had happened at school. "The worst part is, Molly has never even heard of anyone being immune to magic. So, if she is, she had no idea until today. But she did say she felt the tingling sensation I got when I walked through that cloaking spell."

Hands clenched behind his neck, Dad looked at the ceiling as he paced the small space in front of me. How was any of this even possible? I couldn't believe all our plans had been blown apart in one day.

Dad suddenly stopped pacing and stared at me. "Wait. Tray, were you touching Molly when this other girl cast the spell?"

Was I? Hell yeah, I… shit. "Ummm, yeah. I sort of put my hand on her back when they started picking on her. And then this weird protective instinct kicked in, and I tried to pull her out of the way."

Dad groaned and sat down on the stool next to me. "This nightmare just keeps getting worse. It's possible this Molly isn't an Immune at all. The fact that you were touching her when the spell hit means *your* immunity may have protected her."

"What? How is that even possible? Oh God, and I opened my big fat mouth and told Molly all about the possibility of being immune to magic." Okay, now I was sure I was gonna puke, or punch something, or—

Dad's phone started to vibrate on the benchtop, and we shared a look of dread. Surely the news couldn't have spread that fast? Dad's Adam's apple bobbed madly in his throat as he picked up the phone and pressed the receive button.

"Hey Mark, what's up?"

"Can't you call Hill… yeah, okay. I'll be there before then."

Dad ended the call, and I cringed at the look in his eyes. "What?"

"I have to go back to work… and we need to have a long talk."

Molly

"So, how was your day, honey?" Mum asked as she sat down at the dinner table.

My older brother, Ash, looked up from stuffing his face and raised an eyebrow. "Yeah, I hear there's a new guy in your class, *and* you had a showdown with your archenemy, Mandy. So, spill already."

My throat tightened, and I felt the blood drain from my face. Ash wasn't even at school anymore, so how the hell did he know about it?

"*Facebook,*" he said with a wink.

I caught the look Mum and Dad shared from the ends of the table and wished I could just sink into the floor, the sympathy in their eyes making me want to scream. Giving Ash a filthy look, I shrugged and looked down at my plate. "It was just the same ol' same ol'. Mandy said stuff, and I bit. Nothing new."

Ash cleared his throat, and I looked up to find him giving me a weird look as if he were going to say something else. I threw him a total death stare, and he shrugged and went back to eating.

The roast dinner I'd been enjoying suddenly turned to sawdust in my mouth. *What the hell was on Facebook? And who'd put it there?* I pushed my plate away, mumbling an excuse about having homework to do, and left the table. I needed to get to a computer… *now!*

My feet dragged as I climbed the stairs to my room, dreading what I'd find. Had someone posted what really happened at school? Did everyone know I was an even bigger freak? I walked across my bedroom and opened my laptop, clicking on the *Facebook* link. It was one of the few forms of social media that had continued to thrive through the ages, kept alive mainly by the Nothings and the under-thirteens yet to discover their magic.

Holding my breath, I clicked on a new post from one of the boys I knew had been in the bully group. My breath came out in a groan as I started to read.

Did you miss the showdown at Medulla High today? Did Mandy's Magic Malfunction, or did the Nothing Negate her Nemesis?

There were sixty-three comments under the post already. But the gist of the whole thing was that everyone knew Mandy had tried to use magic against me. So, regardless of whether the spell had worked or not, Mandy was in deep trouble.

I breathed a sigh of relief as I read the last post. Nobody believed I could have been immune to the spell. So, Mandy had come out looking like an idiot either way. I was surprised by the number of kids who'd condemned her for being so mean to a Nothing. *Wonders will never cease.*

I closed my laptop and slumped down on my bed. Maybe Tray was right, and the whole thing would just blow over. Mandy must have just botched the spell after all. I closed my eyes and replayed the entire scene in my mind.

Tray's arm slipping around my waist. *Yeah, that part I remembered really well.* Mandy muttering, and then her hand flicking towards me. *Wait... what about the tingling sensation? If Mandy's spell didn't work, then why did I get that?*

I opened my eyes and sat bolt upright on the bed. Nobody on *Facebook* believed I could have resisted the spell. In fact, the word *immune* hadn't even been mentioned. Except by *Tray*. And why wasn't *he* surprised when I told him about the tingling sensation? Tray *knew* way more than he was saying.

My head started to spin with possible scenarios. When I really thought about it, nothing about Tray added up. How did a Nothing know the words to a spell well enough to believe that Mandy hadn't said it wrong? And why would he even *suggest* I was immune to magic, something nobody else appeared to have ever heard of?

I jumped as my phone pinged on the desk. Scrambling to pick it up, I stared at the message from an unknown number.

Have you seen Facebook? Are you okay?

Who is this? I typed back.

Tray.

A shiver ran down my spine. How the hell did he get my number? And why was he so interested in the well-being of someone he'd known less than twenty-four hours? I didn't even know the guy. *Oh God, what if he was a whacko stalker?*

How did you get this no?

There was a long pause before he started to type a reply. Had he been trying to think up a convincible lie?

Long story. Gotta go. Don't mention the tingles or the word immune. Just plead ignorance. CU tomorrow, T.

Great, more questions with no answers. The whole thing was seriously doing my head in. I dropped the phone back onto my desk, climbed off the bed and pulled a pair of PJs out of the drawer. Maybe a shower would help clear my head.

I padded down the hall to the bathroom, my hand on the door handle, when the front doorbell rang. *Weird. It was almost 8 pm on a school night.* Ready to dismiss it as just a visit from one of Ash's friends, I heard the front door open and a deep male voice I didn't recognise.

"Sorry to disturb you so late, Mr Chambers, but we're here to investigate a serious incident that occurred at your daughter Molly's school today. May we come in?"

My heart leapt into my mouth, and the blood in my veins felt like it had turned to ice. Was it just a coincidence that whoever was downstairs had arrived so soon after Tray's messages? It was almost as if he *knew* they were coming. Who the hell *was* this guy?

I was standing frozen at the bathroom door when Mum appeared at the top of the stairs, a worried frown on her face. "You need to come downstairs for a minute, honey. There are some men from the local Mage Council here who need to speak to you."

I nodded, fighting to swallow down the bile rising in my throat as I dropped my PJs on the floor and walked toward her. The tears in her eyes as she pulled me into a hug tore at my heartstrings.

"Why didn't you tell me it'd gotten this bad? I'm so sorry, honey," she said softly.

I hugged her back, rubbing her shoulder. "It's okay, Mum. I can handle it."

She eased me back and held me at arm's length. Up close, I noticed the anger through her tears. "It's not okay. And you shouldn't have to handle this kind of abuse. I'm sorry to say that Mandy deserves everything she gets. Now let's go deal with this."

Mum pulled her shoulders back, turned and walked down the stairs. Taking a deep breath, I followed behind her, the words in Tray's message playing over and over in my head. *Don't mention the word immune or the tingles.* Immune— that had been his word, not mine.

Two men dressed in the official uniform of the Mage Council stood in my living room. The taller one wore a stern, no-nonsense look, while the other had a look of sympathy in his eyes. *Okay, time to play the poor bullied victim.*

"Good evening, Molly. My name is Councillor Douglas, and this is Councillor James. We just need to ask you a few questions about what happened at school today. Would you like to sit down?"

I nodded and moved to the two-seater lounge, my mum hurrying to sit beside me. She grabbed my hand and squeezed it, helping my fear and confusion settle a little. I watched silently as the shorter councillor—James—pulled a miniature tablet from his pocket and began typing.

Douglas focused his eyes on me and cleared his throat. "Okay, before we start, I need you to know that the charges against Ms Sykes for using magic against another person will be quite severe. So, we need you to be completely honest when answering our questions."

I bit my lip and looked down at the hand Mum was holding. I was actually starting to feel sorry for Mandy. She'd been my best friend for years, and now I was going to be responsible for ruining her entire life. Not to mention that I would look like the villain, making my already shitty life even more unbearable. Unless…

I looked straight into Douglas' eyes and tilted my head. "Ummm… excuse me, but *who said* Mandy tried to use magic on me?"

James looked up from the tablet in surprise. He shared a look with Douglas, who scratched his head and looked annoyed.

"Well, we have eyewitnesses who've said…"

"But nobody's asked *me*. Surely, I'd know if someone used magic on me? It may have *looked* like Mandy was going to do it, but she must have come to her senses right before she cast the spell. We said some nasty stuff to each other, and then I walked away.

Seriously, I don't think even *Mandy* would be that dumb."

I didn't miss the corners of James' mouth fighting against curling into a smile before he quickly buried his head in the tablet again, his thumbs moving at the speed of light. Douglas looked like he was about to burst a blood vessel.

"This is a very serious matter, Miss Chambers. Are you sure that's *exactly* what happened? You didn't feel *anything* when Miss Sykes allegedly cast the spell?"

Councillor James was looking at me again, a frown on his face. Tray's warning flashed into my mind. How had he known they'd ask these questions? Thank God I hadn't mentioned the tingling thing.

"Nope. Absolutely nothing. It was just another boring spite session between a Nothing and a Magic. Happens all the time." I fought to keep the bitterness from my voice. Everyone in the room knew how the Nothings were taunted and ridiculed. It had become just a regular part of life.

Douglas scratched his head again and looked at my parents. "It seems the situation may have been misread. I apologise for the intrusion." He turned back to me with a suspicious glare. "If you think of *anything* else relevant to the investigation, please contact the precinct."

Mum was squeezing my hand again, and I squeezed back. Maybe everything really would be okay.

"I'll see you out," my dad said, jumping up from his

seat on the other side of the room. He hadn't said a word throughout the entire exchange.

"Thank you," Douglas answered gruffly. "Good night, ladies. Enjoy the rest of your evening."

I didn't realise I'd been holding my breath until I heard the front door open and close. The air rushed out of me in a loud *whoosh* as the tension began to seep from my body. *Far out! Talk about exhaustion.* I wanted to climb into bed and not get up for a week.

Mum pulled me into another hug. "Oh honey, I'm so proud of you. You could have got Mandy into so much trouble. But you did the right thing and told the truth. I'm so proud of you."

I was glad I had my head on her shoulder so she couldn't see my surprise. She believed the whole story I'd concocted? Man, I must have been convincing. I shuddered at the thought of what might have happened if I'd told the truth or if the spell had worked.

"Thanks, Mum," I said, extricating myself from her arms. "Now, is it okay if I go to bed? It's been a long day, and my head is seriously pounding."

"Of course, honey. Maybe you should have the day off tomorrow. Allow the whole thing to blow over."

"Sounds good," I said as I climbed off the lounge and headed toward my room. I was almost to the stairs when my dad stepped in front of me, a frown on his face.

"What the hell was that all about?" he asked, rubbing his chin. "Those councillors seemed pretty convinced

Mandy used a power thrust against you. They started by asking how badly you'd been hurt, then acted really weird when I said you were fine. It was almost as if they thought you were—"

"*Lance*, Molly has a splitting headache, and I *really* need a coffee," Mum interrupted, almost jumping off the lounge and dragging my dad towards the kitchen. "Goodnight, sweetheart. I'll let the school know you won't be there tomorrow."

Okaaay… now even my parents were acting weird. Mumbling a goodnight, I climbed the stairs for what felt like the hundredth time that day. *What was going on? Had the whole world gone mad? It was as if everyone I knew was keeping secrets from me.*

I got to the bathroom door and decided to forego the shower. Picking up the PJs I'd dropped earlier, I trudged wearily back to my room. Nothing made sense anymore, and my head felt about ready to explode. Changing into my pjs, I practically fell into bed. I noticed my phone flashing with a text when I reached over to turn off my bedside lamp, but I was *way* too drained to care.

Stuff it. I'd check it in the morning.

CHAPTER FIVE

Tray

I sat and stared at my phone after hitting the send button to Molly. *God, what a disaster.* I so wanted to ring her and explain everything, but Dad had insisted he'd handle it. I couldn't believe I'd involved this poor girl I'd known five minutes in the mess that was my life. *What the hell had I been thinking?*

Yeah, well, that was the problem. I'd been too busy *feeling* to think. When I'd walked into the new school that morning, I'd been determined to keep a low profile. I'd planned to put my head down, finish my final year of school, and then find a job a long way from anyone who knew me. But that was all *before* I met Molly.

I couldn't help smiling at the memory of her shooting Mark the douchebag down in flames with her feisty *bite me* comment. And then, checking me out with those eyes that resembled warm, melting chocolate.

Shit, I needed to stop thinking about Molly and focus on what to do if the interview turned to shit. Fates only knew what would happen if Molly mentioned immunes or tingling. But there was nothing I could do until Dad came home.

Groaning in frustration, I decided I needed a distraction. Sitting there thinking about everything that could go wrong was doing my head in. Jumping to my feet, I walked to the living room, flicked on the television and flopped onto the lounge.

My nerves were just about shot by the time I heard Dad's car pull into the driveway. This had started to feel like the longest day of my life. With nausea rolling around in my stomach, I waited for Dad to come in and tell me what had happened. He walked into the living room and stood in front of me, hands on hips and grinning like a lunatic.

"Well, that didn't quite go as I expected."

"Why? What happened?"

"Your new friend certainly has a good head on her shoulders. She denied that the entire incident happened. She claimed that Mandy changed her mind at the last minute and didn't cast the spell. The girl is a genius. I would never have even thought of using that defence."

Relief washed over me as I stared at Dad's face. "She didn't mention anything about being immune?"

Dad chuckled. "Nope. She basically rubbed it in Douglas' face for listening to unfounded gossip. She even claimed she had no idea what all the fuss was about. I'm pretty sure even her parents believed her. Hell, if I didn't know the truth, *I'd* have believed her."

A slow grin spread across my face. "So, it's all over? We can stay?"

"Well, Douglas wasn't happy about ending up with egg on his face, but we have nothing else to go on, so yeah, it looks like we all dodged a bullet. Anyway, I'm off to bed. I have an early start tomorrow."

"Night, Dad... and thanks."

"All in a day's work," Dad replied with a wink as he turned and headed to his room.

My breath came out in a long, slow whoosh. Now all I had to do was explain why the hell I'd even mentioned the word immune and hope Molly wasn't gonna label me a whack job and tell me to take a hike.

Molly

I WOKE to the sound of someone pounding on the front door and checked the time on my phone. 11.30 am. Wow, I couldn't remember the last time I'd slept that late. Pulling the blankets over my head, I waited for someone to answer the door so the pounding would stop. And then I remembered I'd be the only one home at this time on a weekday. Oh well, it wouldn't be anyone I wanted to speak to. I decided to ignore it and was about to roll over and pull the pillow over my head when a voice replaced the pounding.

"Molly? Are you there?"

Bloody hell... Tray. Great, so not only did he know my mobile number, but he also knew where I lived. *Now*, this was really starting to get annoying. It was definitely time to find out what game this guy was playing. Crawling out of bed, I threw on jeans and a T-shirt, stuffing my phone with the still-blinking light into my pocket. Guess I'd need to deal with that next. Then I ran down the stairs and pulled the front door open, ready to give this idiot a piece of my mind. This girl was *not* stalker victim material!

The look on his face when he saw me stopped me in my tracks. His shaggy hair was a mess, and the dark circles under his eyes made him look like he hadn't slept in days. But it was the look of relief on his face as he pulled me into his arms that rendered me speechless.

"Oh, thank God," he breathed against my ear. "I was so worried when you didn't turn up at school."

Releasing me from his embrace, he held me at arm's length, studying my face. "Didn't you get my messages?"

Heat rushed to my face— *and every other part of my body*—at the feel of his arms around me. *Damn, that felt good.* Wait… messages? I remembered the flashing light on my phone from the night before. "Ummm… sorry, I was too stuffed to check my phone."

"Never mind. It's all over now. Everyone at school is talking about it. I can't believe you let that Mandy girl off the hook. But, then again, it was a brilliant way to throw the authorities off your scent."

"My scent? What is it with you? You act like we're involved in some kind of criminal activity. Why would I have a scent?"

He dropped his hands from my arms and stuffed them in his pockets. "Can I come in? I think we need to talk."

"You can say that again," I snapped, not sure I should let him into my house. But then, he really had saved my bacon the previous night with the Mage Council, so I waved him through the door and pointed toward the living room. He walked in, then turned and raised his eyebrows, looking around the room as if waiting to see where I was going to sit. I just folded my arms and continued to lean against the doorframe. Ok, I was *almost* convinced he wasn't a stalker, but I'd decided to stay near the exit just in case. Tray shrugged and flopped down onto the two-seater.

"Okay, so start talking," I said, trying to at least *look* like I was in control of the situation.

Tray dropped his head into his hands and gave a huge sigh. "This is all my fault. I'm so sorry you got caught up in all this crap, Molly."

Now what was he talking about? The guy was obviously delusional. "Ummm… sorry to burst your bubble, but none of this has *anything* to do with you." As far as I could tell, the only part he'd played in the whole mess was being in the wrong place at the wrong time and being there with *me*.

"Look, I know you must think I'm a total nutjob, but just let me explain. I was telling my dad about what happened yesterday—"

"You were telling *who* about it? Are you *insane*? I thought you said not to—"

Tray's hands came up, a sheepish look on his handsome face. "Yeah, I know. Just let me finish… okay? I promise I'll try to answer all your questions. Maybe you should sit down."

"Fine," I snapped, plopping into the chair closest to the door. "But this better be good."

Tray shrugged. "That depends on your interpretation of the term 'good'." He sighed and leaned back in his chair, crossing his ankle over his knee. "Maybe I should explain a few things first. The reason I jumped to the conclusion that you were an Immune is because… well… *I'm* one."

Okay, that was absolutely the *last* thing I'd expected

him to say. My mouth opened and closed, and I imagined I looked like Mandy had the day before.

"Wait, before you say anything. After talking to my dad, I don't think *you* are. I had no idea that my touching someone when magic was used against them would make *them* immune."

"Okay... stop." I needed a minute to absorb everything he was saying before my head exploded. "This is all just too crazy. I've never even *heard* of an *Immune*. As far as I know, you either have magic, or you don't. You're a Magic or a Nothing. End of story."

"Yep. That's what I thought, too, up until about three months ago when I walked straight through a magical shield that should have knocked me out cold. My Dad nearly had a fit. All I felt was a tingling all over, which is why I recognised what you felt yesterday. But Dad reckons you were probably only feeling a projection of what *I* was feeling when the magic hit."

"So why the big secret? What's the problem with being an Immune?"

Tray looked into my eyes, and I flinched at the fear in his. "Because Immunes are considered a threat to the entire structure of the Magical world. They usually *disappear* soon after they're exposed. It's why my dad and I uprooted and moved from the city. Too much risk of exposure."

A cold feeling settled into the pit of my stomach. It was about the damned tingling feeling. "Ummm... Tray. I hate to tell you this, but that wasn't the first time

I'd felt that tingly feeling. I get it every time I think Mr Krock is reading my mind."

"What? No way. You can't be..." Tray's face had drained of all colour. "Wait, did you say Krock can read minds?"

I nodded, unable to get words past the lump in my throat. If what Tray said was right, then Krock must know...

"Magical balls, Molly. We need to get out of here. Even if Krock wasn't sure why he never got any thoughts from you, trying to read me would have given him the same feeling. And even if he didn't know about the existence of Immunes, being from a small town and all, he's bound to ask someone questions about it now that he couldn't read *two* of his students. Do your parents know anything?"

I shook my head, my gut clenching in panic at his words. *What the hell was he talking about? Get out of here and go where? This was all some kind of joke. I was just a Nothing. How could I possibly be a threat to anyone?*

Maybe Tray was just overreacting again. *Wait... how did he know so much about all this stuff anyway?* The questions I needed answered just kept piling up. "Hang on a sec..." I said, trying to make sense of the thoughts scrambling around in my brain. "How does your dad even know all this? And... and... how did you know those Councillors were coming last night? And how the *hell* did you get my phone number and address?"

Tray jumped to his feet and started pacing the

room, his hands raking through his unruly hair. My blood was beginning to boil. Why couldn't he just answer my questions? Surely—

"Dad is a Councillor," he blurted. "He transferred to a job here when we discovered I was an Immune."

Suddenly, everything fell into place. Tray's dad would know better than anyone what was going on, especially what happened to Immunes. It was his job to turn them in. He'd moved here to protect his son and had virtually jumped out of the frying pan and into the fire. And it was all my fault!

"Oh shit, Tray. I'm so sorry. If I hadn't baited Mandy—"

Tray stopped pacing and gave me a weary smile. "No, Molly. This is *not* your fault. How could you be expected to know about any of this? But I don't think my dad is gonna be able to protect both of us. He's told me that once someone is under suspicion, the Council *always* finds a way to expose them."

Great. So, I'm not just a Nothing anymore. Now, I'm an even bigger freak—a Nothing hunted by the government. Wow, my life just keeps getting better and better. "So, what happens now?" I asked, dreading the answer.

"I don't know. I need to talk to my dad. Hopefully, he'll have some answers. But… we won't be able to stay here."

"Seriously? You expect me to just run away with you when I've known you for like… five minutes. For all I know, you could be some psycho maniac trying to lure me away to do who knows what, who knows where! I might just need a *tad* more evidence that all this crap is the truth before I throw my entire life away!"

"Fine, I get that you don't trust me. But you need to understand how serious this is. 'Cos the minute somebody works out that everything you said last night was a pile of crap, they'll be back. So, you need to at least get out of this house."

My false bravado crumbled at the intensity in his eyes. Deep down, I knew he was right about everything. Mandy really had thrown a spell at me, and for some reason, it hadn't worked. But whatever was going on, I did *not* want to be here if and when the authorities came back.

"Fine. What do you suggest I do then?" I cringed at the snarkiness in my voice. I knew this wasn't Tray's fault, but my entire world had been turned upside down, and I was floundering.

Tray's gaze softened. "You know what's funny? This is exactly the way I reacted when Dad told me what was going on. I was totally pissed about having to uproot and move to some hick town in the back of Beyond. I had a life… friends… people I cared about. And all of a sudden, I was some freakazoid who had to be hidden from the authorities. My own father should have turned me in. So, I get it. I really do."

Suddenly I felt like a complete bitch. This wasn't just about me. Tray had already been forced to run once, and this time, he'd be leaving his family as well.

Oh shit... my family. What am I going to tell them? "I'm sorry, Tray. I shouldn't have taken it out on you. I know none of this is your fault; I'm just s-scared." The tears that had been threatening since this whole nightmare began started to slide down my face. Tray moved to the lounge next to me and pulled my face against his shoulder as the sobs burst from my throat.

Why did stuff like this always happen to me? What did I ever do to deserve the crap life kept serving me? I'd always tried to be a good person, resigning myself to the fact that I'd always be a Nothing and accepting my lot in life.

"Hey," Tray said, rubbing my back. "It'll be okay. At least we'll have some company in our misery."

I choked on a sob and suddenly saw the irony in the situation. So, I'd finally met a hot guy who was a Nothing like me, and we were running away together. Sounded like the perfect romantic scenario, except for one small detail. We weren't in love, and neither of us wanted to leave.

I sniffled and lifted my head, blushing at the state of Tray's shirt. The poor guy was soaked. Tray looked down and grinned. "It's an old one anyway."

His grin was contagious, and I found myself smiling up at him. That was when my brain kicked back into gear again, and I realised I was still wrapped in Tray's arms. It felt so warm and safe.

But then I remembered he was only holding me out of sympathy, not because he wanted to. *What else was he supposed to do with a blubbering idiot on his hands?* I blushed and pulled away, shuddering as a feeling of loss washed over me.

Get a grip, girl. You're his problem, *not his* girlfriend.

The grin slipped from Tray's face, and the closed look was back. The tiny hope he'd been holding me because he was attracted to me evaporated. *He was hot, and I definitely was not.* Maybe I needed to make that my new mantra.

Sighing, I straightened my shoulders and tried to pull myself back together. This wasn't getting us anywhere. "Okay, we need a plan. Where's your dad now?"

"At work. I can message him to meet us somewhere. But it can't be at either of our houses, and I don't know the area. Any suggestions?"

We both jumped as Tray's phone pinged with a message. He pulled it from his pocket and read it, turning a sickly shade of white. "Looks like the decision's been made for us. The authorities have spoken to Krock, and they're on their way. Dad wants us to meet him at some abandoned mine just outside town. Do you know where that is?"

I nodded. I had nothing else.

"Cool. We need to go *now!*"

CHAPTER SIX

Molly

*W*hat *in all the magical dung heaps did I think I was doing?* I seriously needed to do a stocktake of my current situation, which would be a challenge since my brain had obviously left the building and taken up residence in cuckoo land. Still, I needed to do *something* normal to ward off the impending heart attack. And I was the queen of assessing a situation and compiling to-do lists.

So… I was currently in a car with a stranger I'd met just over twenty-four hours ago. We were heading to an out-of-the-way deserted mine to meet the stranger's supposed Father. My family had no idea where I was or what was going on. And according to this stranger, I wasn't just a Nothing anymore. I was an *Immune Noth-*

ing. Someone the Mage Council hunted down and *disposed of.*

Yep… this day had already leapt way past the top of my *Days-I-should-have-stayed-in-bed* list. It was now the sole resident on my newly created *I'm-going-to-die-today* lists. Riigghhtt… so maybe taking stock of my situation right now hadn't been the brightest idea after all. Suddenly, I was leaning toward not thinking and giving rein to the numbness now filtering through my body. Much more fitting under the circumstances.

Yeah right. As if that could ever be a viable option for long. In fact, by the time we turned onto the dirt road leading to the old mine, I was convinced the million questions clambering around in my newly returned brain would result in Mum's head explosion I'd imagined the previous day. Tray hadn't said a word since we'd left the house, and the silence needed to end… now!

"Tray? What else did the message from your dad say?"

Tray continued to stare out the window, which made me want to… well… do something to make him pull his head out of his butt. "Nothing… just *Plan B*. We knew this might happen one day. It's why we had to leave Mum and my sister behind when we left Sydney. They needed to maintain plausible deniability."

"I'm so sorry, Tray. That must have been horrible." *Damnit! Maybe it was time I pulled my own head out of* my *butt.* I hadn't even considered how all this would be affecting him. I'd been too busy wallowing in my own personal pity party.

"Mum and Dad had to pretend they were separating due to *irreconcilable differences,*" Tray continued in a dull, pain-filled voice. "All our friends were gobsmacked, saying that Mum and Dad had always seemed so happy... mainly because they *were.*" He groaned. "Fates, what a mess."

We turned a bend, and a white Ford parked on the side of the road ahead came into view, which was when the reality of where I was and what I was doing slammed back into me like an out-of-control freight train. *Why was I feeling sorry for this complete stranger again? What if it wasn't his dad in the other car? What if...?*

Enough! The time for thinking like that was way past. I needed to just suck it up and prepare to deal with whatever was about to happen. Pulling over behind the other car, I sucked in a deep breath.

"Let's go," Tray growled, opening the door and climbing out. "Dad won't have long."

I shivered and did the same, locking my car and then following Tray. I took in the deserted area, nothing but bush for miles. I doubted I'd be able to outrun them even if I got away. At least Tray seemed more concerned with getting to the man stepping out of the other car than with what I was doing. That was a good sign... right?

I looked up at the man stepping out of the Ford driver's side door, and my eyes nearly popped out of my head. I knew that man. It was Councillor James.

The older man smiled and nodded at my surprise. "Hello again, Ms Chambers. I must say I was surprised when the bulletin came in that we were looking for *two* Immunes. From what Tray told me yesterday, not to mention your amazing performance last night, I was convinced you were in the clear. But apparently, your history teacher believed otherwise. I was looking forward to our meeting under different circumstances. Oh, and you can call me Ben." He flashed a sad look at Tray and sighed. "I take it Tray has filled you in?"

"Ummm… he may have forgotten to mention one tiny detail. Like the fact that you're his *dad!* But you don't even have the same surname?"

Tray shrugged. "Yeah, about that. Sorry, Dad and I both use the shortened version of our surname. I opted for Harper because being the son of a Councillor when you're a Nothing just gives the bullies more ammunition." A pained expression flashed across his dad's face, and then the same closed look I'd seen on his son's face fell into place. Now I knew where Tray got it from.

"Much as I'd like to sit and chat, it's way too dangerous for you kids to stay here any longer." Ben reached into the white car and pulled out a backpack that appeared to be almost bursting at the seams, patting the front pocket and handing it to Tray.

"There's money and a new phone in there. I have the number. Molly, I'll need the keys to your car and your phone. I'll make sure they're found a long way from here. Just lay low for a while. I'll message you where to go as soon as I can get the details."

I had so many questions that I didn't even know where to start. From the looks passing between Tray and his dad, I knew there was a hell of a lot they weren't telling me.

Before I could open my mouth, Ben pulled me in for a hug. "Tray will look after you. You just need to trust him," he whispered in my ear.

My first reaction was to stiffen at the weirdness of being hugged by a stranger. But then, I was quickly coming to realise that what constituted as weird may just be becoming the basis of my new normal. This man hugging me was being forced to say goodbye to his son for who knew how long. So, I returned the hug, even if it was a tad awkward.

"I'll try," I whispered back.

Ben nodded and released me, rubbing my arm and giving me a sad smile. He turned to Tray and a groan escaped his lips as he pulled his son in for a hug. Tray immediately dropped the backpack and returned his father's embrace.

Feeling like I was intruding on their moment, I turned away, angry at the unwanted tears welling in my eyes again. *This just plain sucked! All of it!* I hadn't even had time to say goodbye to my own family. The knot in my stomach twisted at the idea that I may never see them again. What would they think when they found me gone?

I turned back and found Tray watching me over his dad's shoulder. He was hurting just as much as me. The last thing he needed was for me to turn into a blubbering idiot again. Blinking away the annoying tears, I pushed all the doubts to the back of my mind and put on a brave face. At least Tray and his dad had now provided all the evidence I needed to believe that what we were doing was the only solution.

Tray gave his dad one more pat on the back and then pushed away to pick up the backpack. "Time to go," he said, holding out his other hand. "You ready?"

The doubts and fears started to push their way to the surface again. *Was I ready? Could I really walk away from everyone I knew and loved and just step into the unknown with this stranger?*

But something in Tray's eyes told me I could trust him. I put my hand in his and he squeezed it, the gentle smile on his face warming me like a ray of sunshine breaking through the clouds. Just for a moment, I allowed myself to believe that everything might be okay.

I STARED out the window as we hit the highway, the reality that I was leaving my home and everyone I'd ever known behind settling in further with every kilometre. An uncomfortable silence hung in the air.

What the hell were we supposed to talk about? We didn't even know each other. I shivered as fear and dread licked its way up my body. *What the hell was I doing here? What if I was making a huge mistake? What if —*

"Hey," Tray said, putting his hand on my arm and snapping me out of my sombre thoughts. "I thought you had like a hundred questions you wanted to ask me."

I shrugged and continued to stare out the window. *What was the point of asking questions? I already knew I wouldn't like any of the answers. Maybe I was better off not knowing. What was that old saying?* Ignorance is bliss. *I totally got that now.*

"C'mon, Molly. Things could be a lot worse?" I knew he was just trying to cajole me out of my dark mood, but seriously?

"Really? And how's that?"

"Well… we could be dead or about to become lab rats."

Lab rats? The fear and dread managed to intensify as

I turned to look at him. *Okay, so maybe I did need some answers.* "Are you saying that's what happens to the Immunes who… *disappear?*"

Tray nodded and shot me a quick glance. "The authorities want to know what makes us tick. Apparently, it's been going on for years."

"But… I thought there weren't many Nothings being born anymore?"

"That's what they want people to believe. It saves them from having to answer questions about why the Nothing population has diminished so drastically over the years. I mean, let's face it. Who cares if a heap of Nothings go missing? We mean about as much to the magical world as the dirt under their feet."

"But why would they bother experimenting on us?"

"Because if enough of us with immunity to their magic banded together, we'd be a serious threat to the Council of Mages."

"So, they're like scared of us?"

"People are always scared of what they don't under-stand," Tray said through gritted teeth. "Plus, they're *supposed* to have everything while we have nothing. It gets right up their noses that we might actually have *something* they don't."

I leaned back in my seat and tried to digest what Tray was telling me. So, the world wasn't just black and white—us and them—as I'd always assumed. There were shades of grey I'd never even considered. I shud-dered at the thought that if I hadn't met Tray, I would have become another statistic in a long line of unexplained disappearances. And my family would have been the only ones to even miss me.

"So, what did your dad mean when he said he'd let us know where to go once he had the information?" I asked, remembering the secretive looks passing between them before we left.

Tray sighed and ran his hand through his hair. "Some of the top dogs in the Mage Council believe the Immunes are planning a rebellion. Dad has been trying to get one of the guys they caught recently to trust him enough to give him the location of somewhere safe we could go. He's hoping that once this guy hears about you and me being exposed, he might finally believe what Dad's been trying to tell him."

We both jumped at the *ping* of a message coming in on a phone. Tray raised an eyebrow and nodded toward the backpack sitting at my feet. "Speak of the devil... can you get that, please?"

I pulled the backpack onto my lap and opened the front compartment. The phone lay flashing beneath a large manila envelope with Tray's name printed on the front. My eyes widened at the thickness of the envelope. *Surely this wasn't all money? How long had his dad been preparing for a situation like this?*

Tray grinned. "That'll be the money. Dad's been stashing it away for years. It was supposed to be for a car for my eighteenth birthday. We were looking forward to walking into the car yard with cash and watching the salesman's face twitch."

How could he continue to look so… *normal?* Here I was, a total basket case over the crap that was happening, and he was acting like this sort of thing happened every day. But then, this wasn't the first time he'd had to run. And he'd had more time to accept the reality of *what* we were. Maybe, given the same time, I'd be the same.

"My parents bought me my Micra, or as I call it, my *little blue rocket*, for my seventeenth birthday. It was out the front of the house with a big bow on the roof when I woke up. I was totally blown away. I had no idea. Best birthday ever."

The possibility of never seeing my family again made my heart ache. I hadn't even had the chance to tell them how much I loved them. To thank them for all the little sacrifices they'd made over the years, trying to make up for the fact that I was a Nothing. Money had never been an issue—

"Aah shit! What the hell was I thinking… or should I say not thinking? I didn't even grab a change of clothes, let alone any money. How could I be such an idiot!"

"Hey, we didn't exactly have a lot of time to spare. Don't stress. We'll get you some clothes before we stop for the night."

"But I don't have any money on me. I don't even have my bag with my keycard."

"Which is a good thing because you couldn't use it anyway. They'll be watching your account."

Of course, they would. Hell, I was such an idiot. Poor Tray must be seriously regretting ever meeting me. I felt like a totally useless burden.

"I'm sorry, Molly. I get that this must be a nightmare for you. But right now, we have bigger issues than who's got what money. Finding somewhere to hide needs to be our main priority. So how about we read the message Dad sent us and go from there?"

The phone. I'd forgotten I was even holding it. Right... it was time to get my shit together and stop acting like a complete moron. Clicking on the message, I quickly read it.

"He says it's all good. Car and phones were disposed of, and he's okay. Wait, why wouldn't he be okay? Ohhh..." I trailed off lamely.

I didn't need Tray to answer my question. I felt like a complete idiot for even asking it in the first place. Of course, the Council would instantly suspect Tray's dad once they found out we were gone. *Wait... What about my family?* Damnit, they'd be under suspicion too. I needed to warn them... I'd just started to key my dad's mobile number into the phone when Tray reached for it.

"You can't ring them, Molly. They'll be fine. They don't know anything. Which is exactly how it needs to stay until after the Interrogator reads their minds and knows they're telling the truth."

"But how will your dad—?"

Tray waved his hand and sniggered. "Don't worry, Dad's an expert at hiding the thoughts in his mind. They'll only be able to read what he wants them to see."

So, I'd done my family a favour by not telling them anything or saying goodbye. Some of the pain and guilt eased from knowing I'd done *something* right for a change.

I was startled out of my thoughts when a familiar tingling sensation ran through my body. I gasped and looked at Tray. Yep, he'd felt it, too. Someone was trying to use magic on us.

"You felt that too, right? Where could it have come from?"

"There's a car behind us that's been following for a while." Panic rifled through me as I looked behind us. A blue car was coming up, fast. "Okay, whatever was supposed to happen didn't, so they know we're Immunes. Hold on, they'll probably try to disable the car next."

Tray put his foot down, and the car took off. I grabbed hold of the dashboard, and the car shuddered under my hands, a tingling sensation running up my arms. *No way! Had I just felt the magic they'd tried to use on the car? But that was impossible.* I held my breath, waiting for the car's engine to die or a tyre to blow, but it seemed to be unaffected. *What the hell was going on?*

"Whoa... how'd you do that?" Tray gasped, looking at me in shock.

"Do what? I didn't do anything. How come the car's still going? I felt the magic hit it."

"Holy shit, Molly. Somehow, you made the car immune, too. That shudder must have been like the tingling we get. That's unbelievable!"

"So, I gather it's not normal for an Immune to be able to do that?"

"Not that I've ever heard. And Dad's never mentioned it. Now I just wish we had a way of disabling *their* car."

I looked down at my still-tingling hands, wondering why it hadn't stopped. The tingling usually stopped after the magic had been used. But then, that was when the magic was directed at me, personally. I'd never been touching an inanimate object when it was hit.

Which was when the most ridiculous thought I'd ever had blasted into my brain. But then, *everything* that had happened in the last twenty-four hours should have been ridiculous. *Aahh, what the hell. It was definitely worth a try.*

Feeling like a complete loon, I turned and pointed at the car that was still following us. I had no idea what I was doing or how magic even worked. But I had to do *something*. I was sick of feeling like a useless burden. Maybe if I just aimed my fingers at the car behind us and tried to push the tingling out of them. So, I just... did it.

The tingling stopped at the same time I heard the

tyres of the other car blow. *Coincidence? Not likely.* Now out of control, the car veered to the other side of the road, hit the embankment and rolled. I sat in my seat, feeling like a stunned mullet. *No way I'd done that. Right...?*

Tray started to laugh, slapping the steering wheel in excitement. "Magic be damned. Now I've seen everything. Did you seriously just do what I think you did?"

My mouth opened and closed, but no words would come out. I looked at my hands, and then the massive grin on Tray's face. Finally, I cracked a smile. He believed I'd done it too. So, if he could even conceive that what I'd done was possible, then maybe I could too.

Tray kept chuckling and shaking his head as we sped away from our would-be captors. Staring at my hands again, I replayed the whole thing in my head. *Wow... who knew, eh?* Maybe the Mage Council *should* be worried about someone like me. 'Cos, to be honest, I was more than a little scared of myself. How many other Nothings out there might have this power? They could go their whole lives without even knowing they're an Immune if no one ever tried to use magic on them. And as for knowing they could do whatever the hell that thing I'd just done was? The possibilities were endless...

I'd noticed that Tray's eyes kept sneaking looks at me as we drove on. He looked to be about to burst from holding back his questions, but he waited a good ten minutes before breaking the silence.

"Are you ready to talk about it yet? 'Cos I am *so* busting to know what just happened."

I took a deep breath and blew it out. Maybe if I said it all out loud, it would feel more real. Because no matter how many times I replayed it in my head, it all still felt like a dream I couldn't wake up from.

Closing my eyes, I started to talk, telling Tray everything I'd felt and done after the magic hit our car. When I was finished, he removed one hand from the steering wheel and lifted my chin. When I opened my eyes, his blue ones were gazing into mine. "You are amazing. You know that, right?"

My face burned at the intensity in his eyes. "Ummm… shouldn't you keep your eyes on the road? I'm not sure how much help I'd be if we actually ran off the road." His hand slipped back to the steering wheel, and he chuckled but kept his eyes glued to the road for a while.

"So… ummm… you don't think this makes me an even bigger freak than I already was?" The words slipped out before I could stop them.

"Are you kidding me? You probably just saved our lives. I'm gobsmacked you even thought to try it," Tray said

"Well, I figured anything was possible, especially after what I've learned recently. Besides, if you don't know what's *impossible*, it doesn't stop you from trying to do… stuff." I threw my hands in the air, feeling stupid at my feeble attempt to explain what I'd done. Sometimes I really wished I could just keep my big mouth shut.

"Y'know, that kinda makes sense in a weird way. Nothing's impossible until you prove it isn't."

We both burst out laughing at the absurdity of our conversation. Maybe it was the stress over the nightmare our lives had become or the fact that we'd evaded capture one more time. But for whatever reason, the laughter was a welcome release from the tension of the last twenty-four hours.

CHAPTER SEVEN

Tray

I finished reading Dad's text and put the phone back down on the console. Looking down at Molly sleeping beside me, I got that weird fluttering sensation in my stomach that came with the overwhelming urge to protect her again. She looked so tired and defenceless, reminding me so much of my baby sister, Emily, that it hurt.

"Hey Molly, you awake? We'll be stopping soon."

She opened her eyes and stretched, her eyes widening in surprise at the glorious sunset on the horizon. She looked at me, and the surprise changed to concern.

"Oh, Tray, why didn't you wake me? You look like you're about ready to fall asleep at the wheel."

I rubbed my eyes, stretching my back until it

cracked. "Nah… I'm fine. But I just pulled over 'cos I got a text from Dad. Knowing where we were headed, he arranged for us to stay in a secluded little house not too far from the last town we went through. He said we should hide the car and stay put until we hear from him. Apparently, our photos are all over the news."

I watched the emotions flitting across her face as I spoke. Her concern for my welfare had been replaced by relief when she learned we finally had somewhere to go. I started the car and pulled back onto the road. We'd been driving for less than five minutes when Molly broke the silence.

"So, how do we find this house?"

"From what Dad said, the turnoff should be just… Wait… that looks like it." I slowed down and turned the car onto a dirt road that looked like it hadn't been used in years.

We crawled at a snail's pace for a couple of kilometres along what quickly degraded into more of a track than a road. I tried to hide my smile at the sight of Molly jumping every time a tree branch scraped against the windows. The sun had almost disappeared when the track began to widen out, and a small house came into view. It was obviously old and run-down, but it felt like we'd reached an oasis in the desert.

I pulled into the shed beside the house, turned off the car and gave Molly a wicked grin. "So whaddya think? Not exactly a five-star motel, but hey… beggars can't be choosers. At least there should be a shower and a bed."

Molly groaned and scrambled out of the car, hurrying toward the front verandah. I'd left the car's headlights on so we could at least get inside the house without killing ourselves. "The key is in the planter to the left of the door", I called, chuckling at her mad dash into the unknown. She scrounged around in the planter, held up the key like she'd won a prize, and then froze, her eyes like saucers.

"Molly... what's wrong?" I raced over to the verandah and reached for her arms, looking frantically around for what might have stopped her in her tracks.

Tears welled up in her beautiful eyes as she bit her bottom lip. "We d-don't have any food. How are we going to survive out here with nothing to eat? We can't go into town because someone might recognise us. Oh Fates, Tray, I'm sorry I'm crying again... but I can't stop."

I pulled her against my chest and wrapped her in my arms. "Hey, it's okay to cry." Rubbing small circles on her back, I rested my chin on her head. "It hasn't exactly been your normal run-of-the-mill day. Besides, I think I may have a solution to the food problem."

Unwilling to break the connection, I took the key from her hand, reached one hand past her, used the key and opened the door, keeping her safely tucked beside me the whole time. Relief washed over me at the smell of something delicious cooking in the oven. *Thanks, Mum.*

Molly stepped out of my arms, looked up at me and gasped. "But… but… how?"

I grabbed her hand and squeezed, leading her through the shabby but clean living room and into an immaculately scrubbed kitchen. Opening the fridge door, I watched her jaw drop. As I'd hoped, it was stuffed to overflowing.

"Ta-da." I waved my hand in front of the open door, a goofy grin on my face. "My mum is a Teleporter. Dad asked her to pop over while we were driving. So, whaddya think? Will this do?"

"Holy shit, Tray. This is unbelievable. Your mum did all this in a couple of hours?"

I looked around and nodded, hit by a pang of sadness at the thought of what Mum and Dad had always done for me. "That's my mum for you," my voice caught, and I sucked in a deep breath. *Okay, I definitely needed some alone time.* "I'll be right back. Forgot the backpack." I turned and headed back out the front door, hoping Molly wouldn't offer to come with me. I guess she understood because she didn't offer.

Molly

GUESSING that Tray needed some time alone, I turned and looked around the small kitchen, the loud grumbling sounds coming from my stomach reminding me I hadn't eaten all day. I opened the oven and nearly passed out at the delicious aroma of freshly cooked lasagne. The day may have been a total nightmare, but my stomach was cheering as if I'd died and gone to heaven.

I grabbed the tea towel hanging on the oven door and lifted the tray out of the oven, dropping it quickly on the benchtop as the heat started to penetrate the towel. Tray's mum obviously hadn't been gone long; the tray was still scorching hot. I quickly located plates and utensils and served a huge helping onto each of our two plates. Man, I was starving.

I was relieved to see Tray walking in the door as I carried the plates to the dinner table. I wasn't sure how long I could have held off eating if I'd had to wait for him. He raised an eyebrow, and I blushed, guessing what was going through his head. *How weird was it to be* playing house *when we'd only just met?* I just shrugged, and he grinned as he sat down at the table. It seemed we'd both decided not to address the elephant in the room.

The only sound for the next five minutes was the scraping of cutlery against plates. The lasagne tasted even better than it smelled, and we both had a second helping. Strangely enough, it was a comfortable silence. Something about sharing the possibility of dying, and then surviving, had removed any tension from the air. *Funny that...*

When my stomach began to protest at the thought of even one more mouthful, I pushed my plate away and leaned back in my chair. Tray seemed to have reached the same point, and he jumped up and took our dirty dishes to the sink.

Opening the fridge door, he pulled out a can of Coke. "Want one?"

"Yes, please."

"I vote we leave the dishes 'til the morning. I think we've earned some downtime. Wanna join me in the living room for a while?"

I nodded and stood up, suddenly nervous about being alone with him again. Giving myself a mental slap, I focused on the friendship that seemed to be developing between us. It had been a long time since I'd had anyone I could call a friend.

Tray eased into one of the recliners and sighed, flipping the leg rest out and crossing his ankles. I was sure my stupid heart skipped a beat as he looked up and gave me a warm smile. "You really should try this. C'mon, I promise I won't bite."

My face burned again when I realised I'd been standing there checking him out like a love-sick puppy. "Ummm... I just want to check out the rest of the house first. Be right back," I muttered, turning and fleeing the room like the total wuss that I was.

There were only two doors off the hallway. I opened one to reveal a bathroom, which meant the other one must be a bedroom. *Hang on...* There was only *one* bedroom? I slowly opened the door and switched on the light, the sight of the four-poster double bed in the middle of the room making me go weak at the knees. *One* bedroom, with only *one* bed. Surely Tray couldn't think—?

As if the thought of him had conjured his presence, his warm hand settled onto the small of my back. "That would explain the fold-out bed in the corner of the living room," he said. and I stepped away from him into the room. I needed him to stop touching me. I was serious about not crossing the line between friends and… well, anything else. The last thing I needed to add to the chaos that had become my life was developing feelings for some guy I just met. *Stop it, Molly, just stop it.*

I dragged my eyes away from the bed and took in the rest of the room. A large bay window looked out onto the forest at the rear of the house, a window seat built into the wall below it. I gasped as I recognised the backpack nestled among a couple of cushions. *What the hell...?*

No way. It had to just be a coincidence that I had the same bag in my cupboard at home. Holding my breath, I crossed the room and unzipped it. Okay, so it couldn't be a coincidence that *my* clothes were in this bag. A small white envelope fell to the floor as I rummaged through the familiar clothing neatly folded inside the bag. Bending to pick up the envelope, I instantly recognised the handwriting on the front. My name was written in Mum's unique flowery script.

I looked across at Tray, my eyes filling with tears—yep, apparently, I was turning into one of *those* girls. "Tray? How…?"

Tray shook his head and stuffed his hands in his pockets. "No idea, sorry. Dad didn't mention this part. Maybe the letter will explain it. I'll be in the living room if you need me." He sighed and then turned and left the room.

I sat down on the window seat and pulled my knees up to my chest, leaning back against the wall and staring at the envelope. My hands shook as I opened it and pulled out the two neatly folded pages. Sucking in a huge breath, I began to read:

My darling Molly,

I can't believe this is happening. I'm so sorry we're not there to help you through this nightmare, but it's a huge relief to know you are safe. No matter what anyone says, I refuse to believe we'll never see each other again. But then, I have always believed in miracles.

I'm sure you're wondering how this bag appeared wherever you are, so I'll fill you in on what's happened since you left. When the Councillors who'd been sent to our house discovered you'd disappeared, Ash, your father and I were immediately 'detained' for questioning. We were surprised to find ourselves in a sitting room with Councillor James, his wife and daughter. It didn't take long to find out it was their son you'd supposedly 'run off with'. Like us, they claimed to know nothing about the whereabouts of either you or their son. As far as we all knew, Tray was at school, and you were at home.

Anyway, after we were all interrogated, and they couldn't find any knowledge of what had happened in our minds, we said goodbye to Councillor James and his family and headed home. I was beside myself with worry until your father pulled me into the bathroom and showed me a note that Councillor James had slipped him when they'd shaken hands goodbye. It explained that you were safe but that you'd had to leave in a hurry with no time to pack a bag or say goodbye. He asked that we pack what you'd need for a while, and he'd make sure it got to you. So, I've packed up what I thought you'd need and want, and here it is. I've no idea how he plans to get it to you, but it's probably best I don't know.

Councillor James has assured us he's doing everything he can to keep you safe and that his son will look after you. Believing that is the only thing keeping me sane right now.

Well, I'd better finish this letter and get it into your bag before it leaves. Just know that we all love you, miss you, and will always be proud of you. And hopefully, one day soon, we'll all be together again.

Copious amounts of love and extreme hugs

Mum xxx

(And love from Dad and Ash, too, of course)

The tears continued to pour down my face and drip off my chin as I refolded the letter and slipped it back into the envelope. I smiled at Mum's use of the words 'copious amounts'. Typical. We'd always loved finding unusual words and seeing what contexts we could use them in. I wondered how long it took her to think up another term for 'heaps of'. She'd known it would bring a smile to my face.

I don't know how long I'd been sitting there reminiscing about my childhood when I heard Tray clearing his throat. Looking up, I found him leaning against the doorframe, his arms folded as he studied me.

"You okay?" he asked gently.

I nodded, trying to conjure up a smile.

"I thought you might have fallen asleep. Do you need anything?"

"No thanks, I'm fine," I said, holding out the letter towards him. "Would you like to read it? Your family is mentioned there, too."

He hesitated, studying my face as if to make sure it was really okay. Whatever he saw must have convinced him because he crossed the room, took the letter and sat down on the bed to read. I wanted nothing more than to just sit and study the expressions on his face as he read, but he'd allowed me my privacy, so I needed to do the same.

I started going through my bag, smiling as I pulled out each item, knowing exactly which things mum would have considered 'needs' and those that were 'wants'. I'd almost reached the bottom when my hand brushed against another envelope. I pulled it out and nearly choked at the thick wad of cash inside. How had they managed to get their hands on so much cash without notice? Nobody had this sort of cash just lying around, except maybe Tray's dad, who'd been planning for a long time.

"Molly? What's up?"

I pulled out the money and grinned at him through watery eyes. Now I wouldn't have to feel like a total burden. I had no idea how much money was there, but at least I could finally pull my own weight.

A sticky note sat on the top of the pile, and I laughed as I read it out loud to Tray:

P.S. Apparently, Ash has been secretly stashing money away for a motorbike. But we decided that you staying safe was way more important. Love you xxx

"Mum would never have let him buy a motorbike, so I guess it was a win-win situation for her," I said, pushing the money and the note back into the envelope. I looked back at Tray, confused by the sadness in his eyes. Why was he sad? He should have been relieved to know I could pay my own way. Maybe something in the letter he'd been reading had upset him.

The look disappeared, and he carefully refolded the letter, stuffing it back in its envelope and handing it back to me. "Well, I'll leave you to get settled in," he said, heading for the door. "You mind if I grab the first shower?"

"No way, Tray."

"What? You want to use the bathroom first?"

"No… I mean, there's no way you're sleeping on the foldout bed in the living room. Your dad organised all of this, and you've been driving all day. You should—"

He stopped and turned back toward me, the cheeky sparkle back in his eyes. "So what? You're suggesting we share the bed?"

Instantly, my face felt like it was on fire again. "What? No! I just thought—"

"It's okay, Molly, I'm just stirring. I knew you meant that you'd sleep on the foldout. But it's not gonna happen. The least I can do after dragging you away from your family and ruining your life is let you have some privacy." He turned to leave again, and I jumped off the window seat and raced for the door to stop him from leaving the room.

Standing in front of him in the doorway, I folded my arms and glared. "Tray, this is *not* your fault. I don't blame you in any way. It was my stupid mouth that got us into trouble."

He stuffed his hands in his pockets and looked at his shoes. "I saw the look of shock on Mandy's face, Molly. You don't usually respond to her jibes, do you? You did it because I was there. If I'd just left you alone and not insisted on walking you to your car, none of this would have happened."

I reached out and put my hand on his arm, forcing him to look at me. "Okay, you're right. I've been ignoring the taunting for years. Mandy *was* shocked that I spoke back to her. But you being there… well, it gave me the courage to stand up to her. It's been a long time since I've had anyone on my side. Besides, it was worth it to see the look on her face." I chuckled, and he broke into a smile. "Actually, it was awesome!"

"Well, I'm glad I could help. Night, Molly, sleep well," he said, then he moved me out of the doorway and headed back to the living room.

CHAPTER EIGHT

Tray

I let out a long breath as I flopped onto the recliner. Damn, that had been close. Turning and walking away from Molly had been harder than it should have been. Her expressive eyes had been practically screaming at me to pull her into my arms and kiss her.

No. I didn't feel that way about her. Our shaky friendship was just starting to develop, and sometimes the line between friendship and attraction could get a little confused. She was scared and vulnerable. I didn't want her to reach for me because I was all she had. I wouldn't cope if there were regret in her eyes tomorrow, in the clear light of day. *Nope, just pull yourself together, man and back the hell off!*

The other thing I needed to consider was the

possible fallout from getting romantically involved and it not working out. It wasn't like we could just move on and avoid each other until the pain of breaking up went away. We were all each other had.

Hell… what if the intensity of her feelings were only a result of the shitty situation we'd found ourselves in? What was that thing where someone falls for their rescuer? Florence Nightingale Syndrome or something. Maybe that was it… she was just grateful for my help.

Whatever it was, I figured friendship was the best way to go. I'd already started to think of Molly as another sister, like Emily.

With another heavy sigh—*yeah, I seemed to be doing a lot of that lately*—I pulled myself out of the chair and rifled through the backpack for some clean clothes. That hot shower I'd been hanging for was way overdue.

Molly

OKAY, it was definitely way past time I put on the brakes where my feelings for Tray were concerned. I walked back over to the window seat, replaying the time I'd spent with Tray in my head. At no time had he shown any sign of being attracted to me. Sure, he'd been kind, and considerate, but how much of that had just been out of sympathy? He felt sorry for me after I'd blabbered on about 'having someone on my side'. I was such an idiot! I seriously needed to get my emotions under control before I made a total fool of myself. There was no way someone like Tray would ever be attracted to someone like me.

The sound of footsteps coming down the hall and a door opening and closing told me he'd gone to have a shower. Right, I needed to pull myself together and *try* to start acting normal. Although, what *was* normal anymore? Well, whatever it was, I needed to get off the emotional roller-coaster I'd been riding since I met Tray and just get on with it.

Brain... it is way past time to reboot! Where the hell was the old super-organised Molly when I needed her? I hadn't even asked Tray what the plan was, how long we'd be here, or if we knew where we were going yet. We were running for our lives, for magic's sake, and I was sitting around creating romantic scenarios in my head. *Idiot!*

Grabbing my pjs and toiletries, I dropped them on the nightstand and decided to repack the rest of my clothes into the backpack. No point in unpacking. We might have to leave in a hurry again, and there was no way I would be unprepared a second time. As soon as I'd finished tidying up, I sat on the bed, waiting for the sound of the shower to stop running.

Yeah, maybe not the best idea. Having nothing to do but sit and listen gave my imagination free rein to think of Tray standing naked in the shower. *Okay, that was weird. Since when did I have thoughts like that? It had to just be a result of our forced close proximity. Right?*

I needed to keep busy. With my nerve endings going haywire, I jumped up and raced to the kitchen. Maybe a cup of tea would help. I filled the kettle and switched it on, relieved to find the new sound blocked out the *other* sound, and its associated images.

I pulled a cup from the cupboard, found the teabags and turned to open the fridge, freezing in midstride, my mouth dropping open. Tray had appeared in the doorway, busily towelling his scraggy hair dry and wearing nothing but a pair of low-slung pyjama pants. He looked up, obviously surprised to find me in the kitchen.

"Mmmm… cup of tea. Brilliant idea. Mind if I join you?"

"I… ummm… the kettle's just… I might just grab a sh-shower first," I blurted, and rushed back to my room, grabbing my stuff and hurrying to the bathroom. How the hell was I supposed to act normal when I was living with a guy who looked like he'd stepped out of a magic-be-damned fashion magazine?

I stood in front of the bathroom mirror and groaned. My eyes were red and puffy from crying, bits of hair had fallen out of my ponytail and were sticking up all over the place, and my face was so red I looked like a god-damned fire truck. No wonder Tray felt sorry for me. I looked like a mangy stray dog.

Sighing, I turned on the shower and stepped under the gushing heat. It felt awesome. If only the water could wash away my thoughts as easily as it cleaned my body. Why couldn't I stop thinking about Tray? It was like I was obsessed with him. To be honest, I'd never really been into boys. *Yeah, but that was because they'd never been into me.* Except for Mark Sykes, of course, but he didn't count. That guy was just plain creepy.

Okay, so maybe *that* was it? After all, Tray was really the first boy who'd ever been nice to me. But whatever was causing these feelings I had developed for him, I needed to stop fixating on how gorgeous he was and start treating him as a friend. Not that I had much experience with *that*, either. Mandy's friendship, the only one I'd ever really had, felt like it had ended an eternity ago.

Fine, what about if I thought of him like a brother then? Now *that* I had experience with. Even though Ash was a Magic, and I was a Nothing, he'd always treated me like his annoying kid sister when we were at home. He'd even stuck up for me a few times over the years when he'd caught someone bullying me. Maybe I could try to be *that* person when I was around Tray? It was definitely worth a try. Because the way things were going, I'd go nuts if I didn't do something.

Feeling better than I had all day, I finished washing the conditioner out of my hair, turned off the shower, and stepped out. I could do this. I just needed to be strong. *No more sooky-la-la-poor-me.* Tray seemed to be a lot like Ash, except he was *way* better looking. I wondered if Tray was close to his own sister. I'd ask him about her when I got the chance.

I walked back out to the kitchen and breathed a sigh of relief at the sight of Tray wearing a T-shirt. He looked at me as if uncertain what to say. God, we really needed to do something about the constant tension in the air.

"Ummm… milk and sugar?" he asked, looking down at the steaming cups.

"Yep, white and one, thanks," I said, smiling. "I know you must be exhausted, but could we maybe talk? About… like… where we go from here?" He stopped pouring the milk and raised an eyebrow, his eyes twinkling. I smacked his arm, and he chuckled. "Don't start that again. You know what I mean… about what your dad's told you and stuff."

He put the milk back in the fridge and handed me my cup. "Sure, I'm wide awake anyway. You wanna grab a recliner? They come highly recommended."

I nodded and headed for the recliner opposite where he'd been sitting earlier, amazed at how much easier things were when I wasn't fixating on my attraction to him. I sat down on the recliner and sighed as I sunk into its comfortable depths.

"You were right. This *is* pretty awesome."

"Sure is." I was relieved to see Tray looking more

relaxed, too. In fact, it was the most relaxed I'd seen him in the short time we'd known each other. "So, what did you wanna know?"

We talked for hours, sipping our tea and learning how to feel comfortable around each other. Basically, all we knew at this stage was that we needed to stay at the house until his dad got back to us. So, we talked about our childhoods, sharing stories of our own personal reactions to finding out we were Nothings. I found myself telling Tray things I'd never shared with anyone. Not that I'd ever had anyone before now who'd understand what being a Nothing was like. Maybe this whole friends thing was just what I'd needed.

I could feel my blinks starting to get longer and longer, and I drifted off to sleep, listening to Tray talk about his sister, how they had always been close, and how I reminded him of her a lot. It seemed the whole brother/sister idea might just work after all.

Tray

I SAT IN THE RECLINER, watching Molly sleep for the second time in twenty-four hours. I'd enjoyed the previous hours sharing stories with her, both surprised and relieved to discover we were alike in more ways than I would have guessed. I'd been drawn to Molly from the moment we met. Everything just seemed to be easier when she was around. There was something special about this girl.

I chuckled as I thought back to what had happened in the car earlier. Somehow, Molly had been able to absorb the magic the Councillors had used on our car and then throw it back at them. How was that even possible? And why hadn't it happened when Mandy threw the spell at her yesterday?

Wait... what if she could only absorb the magic through an inanimate object? That would mean the car had acted as a conduit of sorts. Whoa... just when I'd thought things couldn't get any weirder.

A huge yawn escaped, and I realised how exhausted I was. So, what was I supposed to do now? Should I leave Molly asleep in the recliner and just climb into the fold-up bed? *Ummm... nope, not a hope in hell.* After mentally calculating the space needed to unfold the bed, I knew there was no way it would fit with her recliner in its fully reclined position. Great, I guess I'd have to wake her up.

"Molly... time for bed," I called softly across the room.

Nothing.

Climbing out of my seat, I crossed the room and gently shook her shoulder. "Ummm... Molly, you need to wake up and go to bed. Sleeping in the chair will make you stiff."

"Mmmm... all good. I'm fine..." she mumbled, pushing my hand away.

I grinned and sucked in a deep breath. Okay, desperate times called for desperate measures. Decision made, I bent and scooped her up into my arms, smiling when she slipped her arms around my neck and sighed contentedly against my chest. It was exactly what Emmy used to do when I carried her to bed.

She smiled and snuggled down into her pillow. Unable to resist, I placed a soft kiss on her forehead and left the room. Hey, it had been a brotherly kiss, just another thing I always did when I'd carried Emmy to bed. Besides, there was no rule that said you couldn't be affectionate with your best friend. Which was exactly what Molly was rapidly becoming.

CHAPTER NINE

Molly

The smell of bacon and eggs wafting under the bedroom door hit me before I'd even opened my eyes, and I sat bolt-upright in bed. *Wait... this wasn't my room. Where...?*

Memories of the previous day's events slammed into my brain. *Oh yeah, on the run, hiding out in a house in the middle of who-knows-where with a guy I only just met.* Yeah, okay... I remembered all that. But how the hell was I in the bedroom? The last thing I remembered was falling asleep in the recliner. Shaking my head, I dived out of bed and stumbled to the kitchen. How tired must I have been to not even remember going to bed?

Tray was standing at the cooktop, spatula in hand, as he hummed to himself. Damnit, he looked like he'd just stepped out of a photo shoot, even first thing in the morning! I groaned and flopped down into a chair at the kitchen table. *Oh great, he was a morning person. Something I definitely was not!*

He turned with a disgustingly happy smile and winked at me. "Good morning, sleepyhead. Totally sexy morning look you've got going on there."

Laying my elbows on the table, I dropped my head onto them. If there was one thing I couldn't stand, it was chirpiness first thing in the morning. Forget the brother/sister thing, today he reminded me of my mum.

I jumped at the feel of his warm hand resting on my shoulder, his voice soft in my ear. "White with one, right?" he asked, placing a coffee cup on the table in front of me. He chuckled, and the hand slipped away.

"How do you like your eggs?"

I was seriously going to slap him if he kept up the chirpiness. "Cooked," I muttered, still not lifting my head from the table.

Tray cracked up laughing. "Not a morning person, huh? You're so much like Emmy it's frightening."

I sighed and lifted my head. His sister, Emmy, sounded like a kindred spirit. I wished she was here so she could hold him down while I pummelled him. I giggled at the thought, and he looked over in surprise.

"I'd love to know what *that* thought was about," he said, chuckling as he lifted the bacon and eggs onto the two waiting plates. "Here. Food usually helps

Emmy tame the snarling beast. Maybe it'll work for you too."

Looking down at the plate he'd just placed in front of me, I felt like the biggest bitch ever born. He'd done all this while I'd been sitting here like a disgruntled princess. Tray sat down in the chair opposite, and I felt my cheeks doing the damn burning thing again.

"I'm sorry, Tray. Thanks for all this. I really do appreciate it."

"It's all good. I'll try to keep my morning cheeriness to a minimum, at least until after we've finished eating." He grinned and looked down at his plate, concentrating on eating his breakfast.

I sighed as I picked up my cup, leaning back in my chair and watching him eat. How could he be this cheerful with all the crap going on in our lives? I'd never met anyone with such a positive outlook on life —especially another Nothing. Maybe I needed to take a few lessons from his book.

"Eggs not done right?" he asked, pointing his fork at my plate.

"Oh no, they're perfect. Thanks," I replied, sitting forward in my chair and picking up my knife and fork. Heat rushed to my face again as I looked down at the pile of food on my plate. No way I was admitting that I didn't like to eat as soon as I got up. Not after he'd gone to so much trouble to make things pleasant. The least I could do was eat the damn food. It was obviously time for me to break some long-ingrained habits.

We ate in silence for a couple of minutes, but it wasn't the comfortable silence we'd had at dinner the previous night. I looked up between mouthfuls and caught him watching me. He looked… confused.

"So, how did you sleep? he asked.

"Like a log. I don't even remember going to bed. I must have sleepwalked there or something." Okay, now *he* was definitely blushing. "Wait, did I do something embarrassing?"

"Ummm… no. I just thought you might have remembered…"

"Remembered what?"

"Er… me carrying you to bed."

"What? Why didn't you just wake me up?"

"I tried, but you kept muttering that you were fine where you were. I thought you'd wake up stiff from being in the chair all night, so I picked you up and carried you to bed." He shrugged and played with his fork. "No big deal."

I covered my face with my hands, wishing the floor would open up and swallow me whole. "Seriously? I can't believe you had to do that. You should have just left me there and let me pay the price for my stupidity. I swear I am *so* not this person you've seen for the last couple of days. I hardly ever cry, and I'm usually quite good at taking care of myself. Okay, the *not-a-morning-person* is normal, but the rest… aaargh."

"Molly. It's okay. You've had a helluva lot more stress to deal with than usual, too, remember. Besides," he said, his lips twitching. "The foldout bed wouldn't fit in the room with you in the recliner."

And then we both burst out laughing. I pictured him trying to wake me up and then attempting to open the bed, and I just laughed harder. The tension in the room evaporated. And just like that, I knew that no matter what happened, we'd both be okay. We could do this.

CHAPTER TEN

Tray

We'd been at the house for almost a week and heard nothing from Dad. Although we'd managed to settle into a reasonably normal routine after the initial hiccups, I suspected that Molly might be suffering from cabin fever. We were sitting at the kitchen table having a cuppa when Molly decided to broach the topic of us getting out of there… *for the gazillionth time.*

"Tray. This is seriously starting to drive me crazy. Surely it wouldn't hurt to just send your dad a text? We know that no one else has this number."

I growled and ran my hands through my hair. Which, from the look on Molly's face, was just another habit that was starting to get on her nerves. I got that she was worried—*hell, I was worried too*—but the constant nagging and snapping were seriously doing my head in. "And what if someone else has his phone and they're waiting for us to do just that? Huh? What if they suspect that Dad helped us? We'd just be confirming their suspicions and walking both him and us straight into a trap."

"But… how long are we supposed to wait? We're almost out of food—"

"What is it with you and food? Don't you ever get sick of whinging? Did you ever even take the time to consider that maybe the reason we haven't heard from Dad is because something's happened to him?"

Molly leaned back and stared at me in horror, but I was too damned worked up to care. Gritting my teeth and avoiding eye contact, I stood up and stormed out the front door, slamming it behind me. *I needed air… I needed space… and I needed to know that Dad was okay.*

Bloody hell, calm down, man. I knew none of this was Molly's fault, and I felt like a total jerk for yelling at her like that, but I was pretty close to losing it completely. Why would Dad leave us hanging for this long? Surely, he knew I'd be worried sick. Which was why the idea that something was wrong had started eating away at me.

I didn't know what to do, and I hated this feeling of helplessness. How long should we stay here and wait? If, magic forbid, Dad was out of the picture, what did we do? Where did we go? These questions had been rolling around in my head for the last two days, and I'd been trying to suppress them, so Molly didn't freak out. *Yeah, great job, dufus. You just did an excellent job of making sure she will now.*

Stuff a duck! She probably thought I'd been hiding this angry monster inside all along, and she was stuck here alone with me. *Right, I needed to fix this.* I'd just go back inside and tell her how sorry I was. Dropping my head into my hands, my face burned as I remembered the look on her face when I'd exploded. *Oh, Molly, I'm so sorry...*

I sucked in a deep breath and marched back up to the verandah. I opened the door to find Molly still sitting where I'd left her, staring at the table. She lifted her head and looked at me, and it gutted me to see the tears welling in her eyes.

"I'm sorry..." we both said at the same time. I walked back over and sat down, about to reach for her hand, when she lifted it from the table and held it up to stop me from speaking.

"Me first. Tray, I'm sorry for being such an inconsiderate cow. I promise I'll try to stop whinging—"

"No, I'm the one who should be apologising. I had no right to yell at you like that. I guess we're both just a bit on edge. If we don't hear from Dad by tomorrow—"

I froze as that familiar tingling feeling washed over me. *Someone just tried to use magic on me!* Stomach in knots, I looked at Molly. She was as white as a ghost. "Did you feel that?"

She nodded. "What do we do?"

"Are your hands still tingling?" I asked her, jumping up and locking the front door. She didn't answer. Her mouth was moving, but nothing was coming out. I walked back to the table and grabbed her shoulders. "Molly?"

"Sorry. No, they're not. Why—?"

"Anybody home?" a deep, gravelly voice called from the front yard. I put my finger to my lips and shook my head, then almost jumped out of my skin when the phone in my pocket rang. I pulled it out and stared at the screen. The sender read Dad. *No way. How could Dad know to ring right when there were Magics here?*

Frowning, I pushed the accept button, aware that Molly was holding her breath. "Well, it's about time," said the same gravelly voice as the one from outside. "Sorry about all the theatrics, but we had to make sure this wasn't a set-up. Your dad said you might be needing some help with a little *Immunity* problem. Mind if we come in?"

"Someone with you just used magic. What's with that?" I asked, disgusted to find the hand holding the phone was shaking.

"Well, how else were we supposed to confirm you were Immunes and not some damned Magic taskforce? Think about it. If you weren't Immunes, you'd be out cold about now and definitely not capable of answering a phone."

Okay, he had a point. And I knew that giving whoever was outside his phone was something Dad would do so we'd know we could trust them. I looked down at Molly's pale face and raised my eyebrows in a question. Her eyes were like saucers, but finally, she shrugged and nodded. It wasn't like we really had any other options.

"Fair enough. We'll put the kettle on," I said and ended the call.

Molly

A SLOW GRIN spread across Tray's face as he looked down at me. Seemed his dad had managed to send the cavalry after all. Well, at least the waiting was over. But instead of the overwhelming relief I'd expected to feel, my stomach continued to churn. Suddenly, I wasn't quite so eager to leave our little safe haven. The very thought of our world being tipped upside down yet again made my head spin.

Tray moved to unlock the front door and then stopped and turned back to look at me. "Ummm… maybe don't mention the absorbing magic thing until we get to know them."

I swallowed nervously and nodded. I knew he was right. These people were expecting to find two ordinary, everyday Immunes. And I was quickly learning that being anything outside the 'norm' made others perceive you as a threat. Depending, of course, on their own perception of normal.

I chewed on my lip and sucked in a deep breath as Tray unlocked and opened the door. The sound of heavy boots stepping onto the verandah was followed by the appearance of a scruffy-looking guy standing in the doorway, who was holding his hand out for Tray to shake.

"Sam," he said as Tray shook his outstretched hand. "And this is Tom, Mike and Sarah."

Tray nodded to them and moved back over to where I still sat at the table. I was pretty sure my jelly legs couldn't hold me up if they tried. My heart was pounding as our four would-be rescuers entered the room in single file, their eyes flicking to every corner. They each carried a rifle over their shoulder and remained alert. Probably a symptom of being on the run. I was surprised by how young they all appeared to be. The guy with the gravelly voice, Sam, couldn't be any older than twenty, and the other three looked even younger.

"So, I'm Tray, and this is Molly. You guys want to sit and have a drink, or do we need to get moving?"

"Nah," Sam said, waving his arm toward the lounges and nodding at his friends to let them know they could get comfortable. "We've got a bit of time up our sleeves. That kettle boiled yet?" he asked with a grin.

I looked up from the table and realised he was talking to me. He was smiling, his hazel eyes twinkling as they met mine. Something about the candid acceptance radiating from their depths gave me an overwhelming feeling that I could trust this man, and the stress finally began to seep from my body.

"Ummm… it will be in a minute." *Oh for magic's sake, was I seriously blushing… again?* It had to be because his gaze was so direct and locked on mine. "What would everyone like? Tea, coffee or coke?"

Scrambling to my feet, I headed to the kitchen, relieved to find my shaky legs were finally capable of doing their job. Silent tension hung in the air, so I decided to ask the question I'd been dying to know the answer to.

"So, which one of you is the Magic?" I called over my shoulder, switching on the kettle and pulling cups from the cupboard.

"That would be me," Sarah said from right behind me. I jumped, and she chuckled. "Sorry, I didn't mean to startle you. Just thought I'd offer to give you a hand."

I turned to find Sarah leaning against the sink and smiling. "Oh, ummm, yeah, that'd be great. Would you mind grabbing the cokes from the fridge? I think they were for Tom and… ummm…"

"Mike," she supplied, still smiling as she opened the fridge and pulled out two cans of coke. A stab of envy knifed through me as I noticed how gorgeous she was. Her long black hair was pulled back into a ponytail, and her warm hazel eyes held a sympathetic look. Wait, I was sure those eyes were almost identical to—

"Yep, Sam is my twin brother," she chirped happily, obviously recognising the look on my face.

"Wait… you're twins, but you're a Magic, and he's an Immune? That must make things difficult."

She shrugged, and the smile slipped. "We were seventeen when Sam found out he was an Immune. When we realised he had to run, I insisted on going with him. No way I was going to let him have an adventure like this without me."

"Hey," Sam's gravelly voice interrupted. "Any chance we'll be getting those drinks today?"

Sarah rolled her eyes and took the cokes to Tom and Mike. "You could always make it yourself, Sam, if you're in such a damned hurry," she threw over her shoulder as she came back into the kitchen. Chuckling, I finished making the hot drinks, and we carried them to the table.

"Ahhh… thanks, Molly," Sam said softly as I placed his steaming hot coffee on the table in front of him.

"No worries," I muttered, avoiding his gaze as I sat down opposite him and Tray. I sighed with relief when Sarah sat down on the other side of the table between the two boys. At least I could focus my attention on her, and not on either of the two incredibly good-looking males sitting opposite me.

Phew… I could have sworn the temperature in the room had just gone up ten degrees.

Tray

MAN, the way Sam was looking at Molly was really starting to piss me off. Okay, so maybe I wasn't attracted to her in that way, but I was still her pseudo big brother, which made it my job to warn off riff-raff like this Sam guy appeared to be. He needed to just back the hell off.

"So… you guys been holed up here alone long?" Sam asked, his eyes appearing to brighten when he spotted the fold-up bed in the corner of the living room.

"Almost a week," Molly replied, blushing as she looked down at the table.

"Right. It's pretty unusual for two people from the same school to both turn out to be Immunes. Did you guys grow up together or something?"

Molly laughed, and I ground my teeth. The guy was seriously fishing for information about what was between me and Molly. I slid my hands into my lap to hide my white-knuckled fists. I had no intention of letting him know I wasn't interested. Something about the guy had been rubbing me the wrong way since he'd first set eyes on Molly.

"Actually, I didn't even know Immunes existed until Tray started at my school almost a week ago. Which just happened to be the day I was exposed."

Sam rubbed his jaw and chuckled. "Wow. So, you were total strangers? And you've been stuck here together all this time? Thank the Fates we got here sooner rather than later." His eyes flicked to the fold-out bed again, and my skin crawled at what Sam was insinuating.

Sarah stiffened in the chair next to me and cleared her throat. At least somebody else seemed to be aware of the tension in the air. "Well, this has been great, but I think it's time we got moving. The Magics have been searching for you guys ever since you disappeared, and we are still a long way from home." She looked at Molly and smiled. "Want some help getting your stuff together?"

Molly's eyes flicked from Sarah, to me, to Sam, and then back to Sarah. She blew out a breath and returned Sarah's smile. "Sure. I don't have much to get ready, but I won't knock back the company."

"Cool… let's do it then." Sarah stood up, throwing dirty looks at both Sam and me, before announcing to the room that we should be ready to leave in ten minutes. Tom and Mike, who hadn't said a word since flopping into the recliners, finished their cokes and headed towards the front door, grabbing their rifles and stepping outside.

"Yeah, I'll just throw my stuff together, too," I

muttered, pushing away from the table and heading towards my corner of the living room.

"Hey Sam," Sarah's voice called from the bedroom. "You may as well grab whatever food's left in the kitchen. No point letting free supplies go to waste."

Sam sighed and got to his feet. He looked over, and our eyes met for the first time since we'd all sat down at the table. I could have sworn I saw a hint of a challenge in those eyes. Right, so it was gonna be like that, was it? Fine. I returned the look and nodded as I turned to finish getting my stuff together.

May the best man win!

CHAPTER ELEVEN

Sam

*H*oly shit... *was this Tray guy intense or what?* Okay, so maybe not with everyone. In fact, I got the feeling that his intensity was reserved just for me. Oh well, life was like that.

Finally locating some garbage bags in the kitchen drawers, I began stuffing food into them as I tried to get my head around this latest turn of events. No wonder I'd felt something was hinky about this mission. Except I'd been way off about *what had caused* the hinkiness. I'd been so focused on the possibility of the rescue of a Councillor's son being a set-up that I'd never even considered the girl who'd be with him.

Molly. Wow. This girl stirred feelings in me I'd never expected to feel again. The effect she had on me was so weird that it was almost frightening. Since the moment those warm, burnt-toffee coloured eyes looked up at me, my heart had been like a runaway train. But while I knew Tray had noticed my interest, I didn't think Molly had any idea what was going on. In fact, it felt like she was totally oblivious to both my *and* Tray's feelings.

Wait. What's with all the feelings crap? It was almost a relief to hear that old inner voice throw its *two-cents-worth* in. No way I had the time or energy to consider letting in *any* of the feelings that came with all that romantic type of bullshit.

Molly was just another girl. And just like every girl I'd met since… well, since *her*, I would not give Molly the power to create a distraction in my life. It didn't matter if she was gorgeous and appeared kinda sweet, and innocent. I knew she'd eventually turn out to be just like all the others, a lying, manipulative bitch who could twist reality to suit her own needs. *No. Thanks.*

But what if she was *different? What if Molly was the real deal?* I groaned as my traitorous heart tried to undermine my sensible brain. Hell, I'd only known the girl for five minutes, and she'd already made me all twisted up inside.

But I'd known in a heartbeat that there was something different about Molly. She reminded me of Sarah. Tried to appear tough on the outside but was all soft and gooey on the inside. I just wanted to wrap my arms around her and kiss her silly. Molly, not Sarah, of course.

When the third bag of food and drinks was stuffed to overflowing, I carried them to the front door and looked down the hallway towards where Sarah and Molly had disappeared. *Just stop thinking about her!* Molly needed someone like Tray, the boy-next-door type, not a hardened bitter arsehole like me. It would be best for everyone if I backed off and ignored the feelings she'd aroused. It would all be fine.

Yeah right.

Sarah

I HUSTLED Molly into the bedroom and sat down on her bed. The poor girl stood looking around the room as if she wasn't sure where to start. She looked totally lost.

"Hey… are you okay?" I asked, and her sad eyes met mine.

"To be honest… I really don't know. Was that weird out there, or was it just my imagination?" She flopped down on the bed beside me and dropped her head into her hands.

"Well, if you're referring to the fact that those two

guys were both drooling over you, then it definitely wasn't your imagination."

"But Tray is like my brother. He even told me he thinks of me as his sister. Why would he care what Sam thought about me?"

"Are you serious? You've been here alone together for nearly a week, and he's been treating you like his *sister?* Hell girl, there was nothing brotherly about the way he reacted to Sam flirting with you."

Hang on… had I really just said my brother's name in the same sentence as the word *flirting*. Sam did *not* do flirting. In fact, it was the first time I'd seen him react like that to a girl since—

"You know what?" Molly's voice cut off my thoughts. "This is *so* not the time or place to even be thinking about who's into who and all those other stupid feelings. How about we just get out of here and go somewhere safe? I am *so* not doing this right now."

I had to laugh at the stubborn expression on Molly's face. Even though I wanted to hate her for having two guys fighting over her, there was just something about her that made me like her. Besides, it wasn't like she'd done anything to lead either of them on. In fact, Molly seemed to be totally unaware of the effect she had on people.

"Good idea. Come on, throw your stuff together and let's get out of here."

Okay, so now that Molly had swung into action, I finally got the chance to analyse my own feelings about what had gone down at the table earlier. I'd pretended to be unaffected by Tray's totally gorgeous body. And now that I also knew what a gentleman he'd been by not taking advantage of the situation with Molly, I was seriously close to swooning.

Because if I was being totally honest, the longing for a guy like that to have those kinds of feelings for *me* made my head spin. Maybe I'd read the whole thing wrong, and Tray really was just being a protective big brother type. *Damn... wishful thinking or what?*

"Right, you ready to go kick these guys butts into gear?" Molly said with a grin, throwing her backpack over her shoulder and glancing around the room for anything she might have forgotten.

"Hell yeah," I agreed as we linked arms and headed back out into the testosterone zone. I got the distinct impression that having Molly around was going to spice things up in the Immune community... *big time*.

CHAPTER TWELVE

Tray

*T*hank fate we were finally all in the van and on our way. The long walk from the house to where Sam had stashed the van had provided the perfect opportunity for my mood to go from bad to worse. Sarah and Molly sat close together, giggling and whispering like long-lost partners in crime. As a result of their instant friendship, I hadn't even had a chance to talk to Molly since the others arrived.

Glancing toward where Sam, Tom and Mike sat up front, I caught Sam's eye in the rear-view mirror, and he smirked. *Damn him.* He knew I had a problem with his interest in Molly and obviously had no intention of backing off.

Fine, I needed a distraction to keep my mind off the entire situation. Maybe it was time to dig for some information about where we were going and what to expect. I decided to ask Sarah rather than any of the *cavemen* in the front seat.

"So, Sarah. What can you tell us about where we're going?"

Both girls' heads swivelled toward me, and Sarah's eyes lit up. "Have you ever been to Lightning Ridge?"

Molly frowned. "What? The place where half the houses are underground because it's like fifty degrees all the time?"

Sarah grinned and nodded. "Yep. Where better to hide a large group of runaways? Except we don't live in houses. We live in an abandoned Opal mine."

"You mean… like… underground?" Molly's frown had turned into a look of abject horror.

I moved across the van and slipped an arm around her shoulders. "Hey… are you okay?"

"There's no way I can live underground. I don't do well in confined spaces with limited air," Molly said, her raspy voice little more than a whisper.

"Oh no, Molly. Please don't tell me you get claustrophobia?"

She nodded and looked up at me, those damn tears glistening in her eyes again. "I did try to warn you I'd be a useless piece of baggage. Maybe you should just tell Sam to pull over, and you can drop me off here."

"Everything okay back there?" Sam's voice interrupted, and I wasn't sure whether it was because he'd heard his name or that he was pissed I had my arm around Molly.

"Yep, all good. How long 'til we get a toilet break?" Sarah asked, smiling at her frowning brother's reflection in the rear-view mirror. Sam's suspicious eyes flicked to mine as he mumbled something about having to hold on.

I looked at Sarah over the top of Molly's head and raised an eyebrow. Why was she hiding Molly's secret when we all knew the huge problem it would present when we reached the Immune community?

Sarah ignored my question and stayed focused on Molly. "Listen, Molly. There's nothing small or confined about the mine where we live. It's really spacious and airy. You'd never even know we were underground once you get in there." Sarah was obviously trying to talk Molly down from the ledge she was teetering on.

Molly just snorted. "You mean, except for the fact that I know we're surrounded by layers and layers of rocks and dirt?"

Sam's gritty voice interrupted the conversation. "Okay, we're about ten kilometres outside the city. Sarah, time for you to drive."

"Why do you need to drive in the city?" I asked.

"Lots of the traffic lights in the cities have magic detectors. If the driver is an Immune, they're instantly stuffed." Disgust laced Sarah's words.

Seriously? Why hadn't Dad ever told me about this

kind of crap? Okay, Medulla didn't have traffic lights, so maybe he didn't think I'd ever need to know. But… well…Shit. What else didn't I know about how badly the Council wanted to get their hands on Immunes?

Sam pulled over to the side of the road, and he, Tom and Mike jumped out and came around to open the side door of the van. Sarah patted Molly's hand and crawled out the door, waiting for the three guys to crawl in and throwing me a smile as she slid the door shut.

Sam glared at the arm I still had around Molly, and I smirked like he'd done earlier. He shrugged and wiggled backwards until his back was against the side wall of the van. "Best we all get comfortable. It should only be an hour or so until we're through the city and out the other side again."

Then he slumped down into the corner opposite us and closed his eyes. I guessed that with an eight-hour drive ahead of us, it made sense to grab some rest while he could. Molly sighed and snuggled in closer, leaning her head on my shoulder. I couldn't help smiling when I caught Sam opening one eye and muttering under his breath.

Tray-1: Sam-Nil. For now…

Molly

THERE WAS no way I could go to sleep. Between knowing I was apparently the reason Tray and Sam kept looking daggers at each other, and the horror at the idea of having to live underground, my head was spinning. *Why did everything in my life always have to turn into a complete shit show?*

I had to admit that I was enjoying the feeling of being tucked safely against Tray. "Don't worry. We'll sort it all out somehow," he said softly. His breath tickled my ear, and a shiver ran through me. I nodded and snuggled in a little closer. Being in Tray's arms made me feel safe and cared for, but I knew Sarah was wrong about what she thought Tray felt for me. Which meant the tension between Sam and Tray was for an entirely different reason. What that reason was I had no idea.

I looked over at Sam, who was still scowling even with his eyes closed, and sighed. I'd promised myself only hours ago that I wouldn't allow any romantic feelings into my already traumatised brain. I had enough other crap to deal with, like staying alive. Oh, and staying sane at the thought of living under tons and tons of rock.

"Ummm... you might want to get under cover." Sarah's voice sounded nervous. "A Councillor with a patrol car is pulling people over up ahead."

Tray immediately pulled me down to the floor

beside him and grabbed one of the heavy woollen blankets scattered around the back of the van. Sam, Tom and Mike did the same, and then there was silence as the van slowed to a halt.

I froze as the heavy blanket settled over my head. This wasn't like pulling the covers over my head in bed. It was more like being trapped under something and unable to get away. *Damn this claustrophobic feeling.* My brain *knew* I wasn't going to suffocate, but it refused to send that message to my body.

Suddenly, I became conscious of the amount of people crammed in the small area of the van, and panic washed over me. *For magic's sake... not now.* But it was too late. I started to shake, my heart hammering in my chest, the urge to throw off the blanket and suck in a deep lungful of air so strong I wanted to scream.

There's not enough air... I can't breathe!

"Sshh, Moll. It's ok, sweetheart." Tray's lips were against my ear, whispering the words softly. "Just breathe with me. Concentrate on my heartbeat and my breathing. In… out… in…out."

I closed my eyes and focused on his words, the feel of his strong, steady heartbeat comforting under my cheek. *Okay... I could do this.* I *had* to do this. Trying to ignore my body's irrational response, I focused all my attention on Tray's arms wrapped around me, his soothing voice in my ear.

The whirring sound of Sarah lowering her window

was a weirdly welcome distraction, and I tried to take in what was going on.

"Morning Councillor. What's up?"

"Searching for a couple of escaped criminals. We'll need to search your van. Please step out of the vehicle and open the back door."

"Ummm… I'm not sure you'll want to do that. There's no way anyone could be hiding in *this* van. I have three dogs back there who don't particularly like strangers."

The Councillor sucked in a breath. "Crikey, could you at least tell 'em to shut up? That barking could wake the dead."

Sarah giggled. "Yeah, like I said. Stranger at the door. Now, you don't really want to mess with them, do you?"

"You're right, I'm sure everything's fine. You have a nice day, miss." The Councillor's voice sounded confused as if he wasn't sure why he'd agreed with her. But a few seconds later, he'd backed away from the van. Then Sarah's window went back up, and we were on our way.

Tray quickly threw the blanket off, and I sat up, dragging air into my grateful lungs. Before anyone could say a word, Sarah burst out laughing, hitting the steering wheel and jiggling in her seat. "Hot damn," she sputtered. "Am I good or what?"

"What the hell just happened? How did you talk that

guy out of looking in the back? Did he really hear imaginary dogs barking?" Tray asked.

Sam, Tom and Mike were chuckling and shaking their heads. "Sarah's magical abilities are pretty spectacular," Sam bragged, reaching over and patting his sister on the shoulder. "Among other things, she can cast illusions inside people's heads, so they only see and hear what she wants them to."

"Yep. That Councillor looked in the window to see three snarling Doberman's hoping to take his head off and decided to back off." Sarah grinned, beaming with pride as she continued to drive out of the city.

"You okay?" Tray leaned forward and whispered into my ear, his hand rubbing small soothing circles on my back.

I turned and smiled up into his kind blue eyes. Actually, I was surprised by how much he'd helped. "Yes, thanks to you. Sorry, I'm such a basket case."

"Anytime, and you're not a basket case."

"Okay, Sarah," Sam growled. "I need to be doing something useful. Pull over where you can, and we'll swap back."

I looked over to find Sam's brooding eyes studying me. *What was his problem?* I leaned back against Tray and closed my eyes, shutting out the questions in his. Suddenly, even without the blanket over my face, it felt like all the air had been sucked out of the van.

CHAPTER THIRTEEN

Sam

*O*kay, *so maybe it wouldn't all be fine.*

Sitting in the back, watching Tray and Molly together, had my stomach in knots. What the hell was wrong with me? I wanted to like Tray; he seemed like a good guy. But every time I thought of him with Molly, I wanted to beat the crap out of him. *Fates help me.* I needed to get out of this insanity bubble and back to base. Then, I could focus on the real world and let all this other magical dung go.

Yeah right... like hiding in an underground community was the real world. Watching Sarah sleeping peacefully on the other side of the van caused the usual guilt to raise its ugly head. She didn't have to live like this. She was a Magic, damnit. She should have been out partying with her Magic friends and enjoying life. I should never have agreed to let her come with me when I ran.

The guilt always came with the gut-wrenching memory of the looks on our parents' faces when Sarah announced she was coming with me. Nothing anybody said would change her mind. Dad looked like he wanted to kill me, and Mum's eyes were so filled with pain that it felt like my heart was being ripped out of my chest. Did they honestly believe I'd done any of it on purpose? Being born a freak definitely hadn't been part of *my* life plan, either.

I growled as an image of Rebecca slipped into my mind. I hated that any memory of home always seemed to include her. I guess because she'd been like part of the family for years. I sucked in a deep breath and realised the grip I had on the steering wheel was making my knuckles turn white. Even after nearly three years, my chest still tightened at the memory of her betrayal.

"How long now? I really need to go." Sarah's voice floated over from the back of the van, pulling me out of my thoughts.

"Hey, sleepyhead. We're about two hours out. There's a petrol station coming up in about ten kilometres. I need to fuel up, so you can use the ladies' room."

"Thank the Fates for that." My heart jumped as Molly's sleepy voice hit me. *Shit. I seriously needed to get a handle on this.* I'd hoped the memories of Rebecca would stomp all over my reaction to Molly.

No such luck. *Damn, I was in worse trouble than I'd thought.*

Sarah

THANK GOD, we were finally home. I chuckled at the image of what I now associated with the word *home,* remembering the horror I'd felt the first time I set eyes on it. My heart went out to Tray and Molly as I watched their faces taking it all in. I *knew* what they were feeling, wondering if they could have done *anything* different to avoid this fate.

Then I remembered laughing at the thought of anyone *ever* considering this stifling, barren, wasteland home. I reached out to touch Molly's arm, pulling back when she flinched. I got why she did it and couldn't help cringing at the look of fear on her face. Glancing at Tray over her shoulder, I could see the worry etched into his face. How the hell could we expect Molly to even go in there, let alone live there?

"So, this is it, huh?" Tray said, trying and failing to sound positive.

"*Oh, no, no, no...* You don't seriously expect me to go in *there?* I'm sorry, but... *no way.*"

I caught Sam's raised eyebrow and questioning eyes in the rear-view mirror. Okay, it was time to bring my brother up to speed.

"Hang in there, Molly. I have an idea. Just give me five minutes," I said, looking at Sam and tilting my head towards outside as I scrambled out of the van.

I grabbed Sam's arm as soon as he stepped out of the van, intent on dragging him out of hearing distance. I already knew he'd explode, and hearing him rant was the last thing Molly needed right now.

After managing three steps, Sam planted his feet and stood in front of me, his arms folded in front of his chest. "Okay, so what was that all about? What's up with Molly?"

"Sam, please don't get angry. I know I should have told you when she first mentioned it—"

"Sar-ah?" Damn, I hated it when he did that. Dragging my name out and scowling like that had never boded well.

"Fine. Molly gets claustrophobia." I closed my eyes and held my breath, bracing for the inevitable explosion. After five seconds of silence, I opened one eye, and my jaw dropped. Instead of being furious, Sam was looking towards the van with—wait... was that seriously longing? *Oh, magic's balls, no.* Sam hadn't just been playing back at the house. He'd really fallen for Molly. I hadn't seen that look on his face since Rebecca.

Ah, shit. Why did I get the awful feeling that this was *not* going to end well?

Tray

THIS WAS WAY WORSE *than I could ever have imagined!* I mean, I don't know exactly what I'd expected an abandoned mine in the middle of nowhere to look like, but the reality *way* exceeded my worst possible case scenario. Molly was already starting to hyperventilate just at the *thought* of stepping into what she must perceive as her greatest nightmare. There was no way I could expect her to go through with this.

"Molly… it's okay. I'll tell them we're not staying. We can find somewhere else to go."

Molly's head swivelled to look at me, a flash of hope in her eyes. But then she sagged and shook her head. "No Tray. There *is* nowhere else to go. Your dad went to all this trouble to make sure you'd be safe, and I am *not* going to be responsible for stuffing that up. Damnit, if I wasn't a stupid Immune, Sarah could cast an illusion on me and make me think the inside of the mine was a wide, open space."

"Ummm, Molly. I hate to tell you this, but if we weren't Immunes, we wouldn't be here." She almost smiled, and I could feel her breathing slowing.

"Seriously though, there has to be another way." I

looked out at where Sam and Sarah were talking, surprised by Sam's worried frown. I expected him to be furious with Sarah for not telling him about Molly's problem hours ago. To be honest, I'd half expected him to send Sarah back to the van and tell us to take a hike. I had to admit, in his place, I might have considered doing the same thing. I was sure he had enough to deal with without worrying about a couple of ungrateful strangers who didn't appreciate the hospitality on offer.

Molly stiffened, and I looked up to see Sarah walking back to the van. Okay, this was it. But when Sarah's face broke into a smile, I released the breath I hadn't realised I'd been holding and knew she had a plan. Behind Sarah, I could see Sam battling to tear his eyes away from the van as Tom and Mike started talking to him.

"Okay, Sam has agreed to give my plan a go. I've no idea if it will work, but it's worth a try. I've heard about people getting over this kind of thing by desensitising themselves to their problems. Maybe we could start with short visits to the mine. So, you don't go in there thinking you're trapped and have to stay. Sam suggested you might want to sleep in the van to start with, or we could set up a tent out here somewhere and slowly build up the time you spend underground. How does that sound?

Molly's only answer was to throw her arms around Sarah's neck and burst into tears. Sarah's beautiful smile lit up her face as our eyes connected over Molly's shoulder. I mouthed *thank you,* and she looked away, blushing. I was so glad Molly had found a friend with such a beautiful heart. Sarah was every bit as beautiful on the inside as she was on the outside.

"Thank you, Sarah. I promise to work really hard at the whole desensitising thing. And if I'm taking too long, one of you just needs to hit me over the head and tell me to get over it." Molly somehow managed to talk, laugh, and cry at the same time.

"I'm sure one of us will come up with a solution. Right Tray?" Sarah's eyes twinkled with mischief, and I was suddenly caught in their depths. Her raven hair fell across her face as she looked away and blushed again.

Stop it, Tray. Sarah was a Magic. As if she'd ever be interested in a plain old Immune like me. She was obviously just trying to be nice. But that didn't stop me from appreciating how stunning she was. *I mean, just wow…*

CHAPTER FOURTEEN

Molly

A shiver ran over me as I stared at the entrance to the mine. Tray and I had slept in the van the previous night—just like any good brother and sister would do—and now I was ready to just go inside for a look. I didn't have to stay in there. I could come straight back out if it were too much.

Tray and Sarah each held one of my hands, and I sucked in a deep breath as I took the first step towards conquering my greatest fear.

Tray squeezed my hand, and I looked into his soulful eyes. "Nothing to fear but fear itself. I won't let anything happen to you. Do you trust me?"

I nodded and returned the squeeze. "Now, can we please just get this over with?"

"Okay, if you were a Magic, you'd be looking at a

projected holograph of a solid wall. I know you guys can just see the entrance, but it might feel weird stepping through the magic the first time." Sarah's voice had a calming quality to it. I suppressed a nervous giggle at the thought of how good she'd be as a tour guide. "The entrance leads to twenty stairs cut into the rock heading down, with a handrail on your left. As soon as we get to the bottom, we're in the main shaft, which is huge. Damnit, I so wish I could just project an illusion into your head so you don't have to go through this."

"That makes two of us. But it's not gonna happen, so we can both wish until we're blue in the face. Now. Less talk, more action." My heart hammered loudly inside my chest; my throat so dry I could hardly swallow. *You can do this, Molly, one foot after the other.*

Sarah dropped my hand and stepped ahead of us, and when we followed, I felt the tingling sensation I'd come to associate with someone using magic on me. I was glad Sarah had thought to warn us about the holograph.

I froze at the stairs leading down from the narrow, rock entrance, fighting the urge to turn and run. And then Tray's arm slipped around my waist, his voice in my ear, his warm breath a welcome distraction. "Grab the handrail and focus on me. We'll be there before you know it."

I nodded and forced my hand to grasp the smooth metallic handrail. *One. Foot. After. The. Other.*

"Good girl. Now, just count to twenty." Tray made it sound so simple. *If only.* I started walking and counting, sure my heart was going to explode out of my chest as I moved further into the bowels of the earth. *Bloody hell... what if the walls caved in? What if there wasn't enough air? What if—*

"Molly. Stop overthinking it. Look, you can see the cavern opening up at the bottom." Without thinking, I moved my legs a bit quicker, anything to get out of what was starting to feel like a coffin. And then we were there...

Magic-on-a-stick. The place was humungous. There must have been easily fifty people down here, sitting around laughing and chatting as if they didn't have a care in the world. A few stopped talking and stared, and I felt my face turning red. It was just like the first day of school all over again.

"So far so good. Come on, I'll show you around," Sarah said, linking her arm with mine and dragging me towards the groups of tables and chairs randomly set up in front of tents.

"How are you doing?" Tray whispered in my ear, and I realised that, for a moment, I'd actually forgotten where I was. Watching all these people act like everything was normal had temporarily suspended reality. If I could just keep the thought of the rock surrounding us on all sides locked away, I might just survive.

"Hey Molly, Tray. Glad you could make it." Sam stood in front of me, his eyes searching for the panic we all knew wasn't far away. I managed a weak smile, and he nodded as if satisfied for the moment. "Kettle's boiled… come join us for a coffee."

With Sarah's arm tugging me to follow Sam, Tray's arm slipped from around my waist. I looked up at him in panic, and he smiled and grabbed my hand. "Don't worry. I'm not going anywhere. We're a team, remember?"

Tom and the pretty blonde he was snuggled up to shuffled along the bench seat to make room for Tray and me to join them. Two steaming cups of coffee appeared on the table in front of us, and Sarah squeezed my shoulder before moving to the other side of the table with her own cup.

"So, everyone, this is Molly and Tray," Sarah announced, smiling at us. "You guys already know Mike, Sam and Tom, and this is Katy." The pretty blonde smiled and nodded. I looked across the table to find Sam and Mike with their heads together, talking quietly. Mike looked over and smiled, and Sam lifted a hand in acknowledgement, although I noticed he didn't make eye contact.

I added milk and sugar to my coffee, sighing as the first sip of warm liquid hit my parched throat. I kept my focus on the table and the people sitting around it, determined not to think about where I was. Maybe I could do this after all.

And that's when it all turned to shit… as usual. A guy at the next table yelled at someone, jumping up out of his chair and sending it flying backwards to slam into the rock wall. A cloud of dust and small pieces of gravel floated into the air, and my world began to spin out of control. Suddenly, the walls were closing in. I was choking on the dust, convinced the unstable walls were about to cave in.

Shit. Shit. Shit. I had to get out of here. I didn't want to die.

Jumping up from the table, I looked around, panic making the dust in my throat worse and constricting my breathing. *Where the hell were the damn stairs?* Sweat poured down my face, my heart ready to jump out of my chest. *What the hell was I even doing here?* Tray reached for me, but it was too late. This was all his fault. *He'd* been the one to make me come down here. I pushed him away and moved out of his reach.

The silence in the air was deafening, and I felt everyone staring at me. But I didn't care. I was never coming back here again, so why would I care what they thought of the crazy new girl?

I could feel the scream rising in my throat, and I was panting, unable to get enough air. *Why couldn't someone just show me the damn way out?* My legs were shaking so badly they wouldn't be able to hold me up much longer. Tears merged with the sweat pouring down my face, and black spots danced before my eyes. *Oh Fates, I was dying.*

"Please…" And then the walls closed in, and the ground rose up to meet me as I fell.

Sam

I WATCHED the scene unfold in front of me; my fists clenched in frustration that I couldn't do anything to stop Molly's worst nightmare from spinning out of control. I'd tried to tell Sarah this wouldn't work, but she'd been so determined that I'd given in. Now, I'd have to pick up the pieces of the disaster I'd already predicted.

Molly's cry galvanised me into action. *Damn it.* I couldn't just sit here and watch any longer. I jumped up and caught her just before she hit the ground, growling at the faces of my friends staring at me. Okay, so maybe it wasn't exactly normal for me to get involved in something like this, but someone had to do it.

I picked Molly up and cradled her against my chest. Sarah had told me that part of the desensitisation process was to make her stay and face her fears until the symptoms started to subside before taking her back outside. But how could I keep her here and let her wake up inside the same nightmare she'd been living when she'd passed out?

I could feel Tray's eyes shooting daggers at me as I

stood undecided with Molly in my arms. Finally, he stepped forward and tried to take her out of my arms. "Thanks, but I'll take it from here. I need to get her out of here." He spoke in a calm but firm voice.

Every part of me wanted to tell him to back off. If he cared about Molly so much, why hadn't he been the one to catch her when she was falling? Huh? Because she'd pushed him away! She hadn't wanted his help. And now it was my turn to try and help her. I'd just opened my mouth to argue with him when Sarah appeared beside him.

"Tray," Sarah put her hand on his outstretched arm. "When Molly wakes up, she needs to be still down here so she can start dealing with her fears. If she wakes up outside, there's no way we'll ever get her back down here because she'll believe her fear was justified. I know you want to help, but maybe it's best if you're not the one making her stay. She'll be irrational and angry when she finds out she's still underground, and Sam has dealt with more than a few traumatised cases."

Tray's eyes swivelled from me to Sarah, and I braced myself for the outburst. But surprisingly, Tray shook his head; his shoulders slumped as his ice-blue eyes burned into mine. "Hurt her, and I'll kill you," he growled through gritted teeth before turning away and shuffling back to his seat at the table.

I breathed a sigh of relief and looked around for somewhere pleasant for Molly to wake up. Preferably that *somewhere* needed to be where she couldn't see the rock walls surrounding her. *My tent*, Sarah mouthed as if she knew what I was thinking. I smiled and nodded, knowing that Sarah's bohemian-style tent was the perfect place for Molly to regain her bearings. Turning away from all the people looking at me like I'd lost my marbles, I headed for Sarah's tent, pushing aside the gaudy floral fabric floating in the doorway.

I placed Molly gently onto Sarah's mattress on the floor, then sat down on the floor beside her. I had no idea what state she'd be in when she woke up, but I had a feeling it wouldn't be pretty. As if on cue, a soft moan escaped her lips, and her eyes fluttered open. She frowned as she took in her unfamiliar surroundings, the crystals and wind-chimes floating above her, the soft, floaty fabrics draped around the walls. Finally, her eyes landed on me sitting beside her, and they widened. I could read it on her face when the memories came flooding back, and she bolted upright on the bed.

"Wh-where am I?" she asked, her eyes flicking wildly around the tent.

"Somewhere safe. Would you like a drink of water?" She nodded, her eyes wary, as I reached for an unopened bottle of water from the shelf, twisted the top off, and handed it to her.

I watched as she emptied half the bottle in one gulp before handing it back to me. "Thanks. Where's Tray? Why isn't *he* here?"

"He's just outside talking to Sarah. He'll be here in a minute."

"Okay. And where exactly is *just outside*? Where the hell am I?"

"You're in Sarah's tent."

"You mean I'm still underground? What the hell?" A trickle of sweat ran down the side of her face, her breaths coming out in short pants, her eyes fixed on the exit to the tent. *Come on, Sam, do something. You're supposed to be helping her.*

"Molly. You're safe. There's nothing here that can hurt you."

"But... you said if I couldn't handle it, I could leave. Why did you make me stay down here? I c-can't do this. I don't *want* to do this. Any of it. I have to get out of here."

I grabbed her hand as she tried to push past me. She flinched and lashed out with her other hand, connecting with my jaw. Then her face froze in horror at what she'd done, and she started to sob.

"P-please... just l-let me go. I don't want to hurt you. I just need—"

I clasped her other hand in mine and pulled her into my lap. She was shaking so badly I could hear her teeth chattering. I wrapped my arms around her, and she buried her head against my chest, continuing to sob and gasp for air.

"Molly... I need you to listen to me. Please...just close your eyes and focus on my voice. Did you ever go camping with your family as a kid? We used to go to this great place and pitch our tents on the grass beside a river. This is the same tent Sarah took every year. That's where you are now... inside Sarah's tent beside that river. Can you see it?"

She sucked in a breath and finally nodded. *Thank Fates.* Maybe she wouldn't end up hating me after all. I brushed the wet hair back from her sweaty forehead and sighed. Small steps. I *needed* to help this beautiful girl overcome her fear because, suddenly, the thought of her leaving made my chest hurt.

CHAPTER FIFTEEN

Sarah

$\mathcal{I}$ watched as Sam carried Molly inside my tent, then sucked in a deep breath and walked back to the table. Tray looked so lost that I decided to slip into the seat beside him where Molly had been sitting earlier.

"You did the right thing, Tray. Molly won't be happy with the person who tells her she can't leave yet. I'm sorry this is all so hard."

Tray turned toward me, and I gasped at the pain in his eyes. "I just feel like it's all my fault. Molly wouldn't even be here if I hadn't tried to befriend her on my first day at her school."

"Oh, Tray, none of this is your fault. To be honest, I think Molly was lucky to have you there when she was exposed as an Immune. I've seen kids arrive here an absolute mess because they've had to go through it all alone. Besides, it's not like you *made* Molly an Immune. She was always going to be at risk of being discovered."

Some of the pain faded from Tray's beautiful blue eyes, and my heart skipped a beat when his lips almost formed a smile. "Thanks, Sarah. I guess I've been so busy beating myself up about being the one to tear Molly away from her family that I lost track of the reasons this is all happening. We were all just born victims of a society that sucks."

"You got that right. When I first got my magic, and we found out Sam was a Nothing, I was so angry I wanted to rip the world apart. Actually, I think Sam handled the news better than me. We'd always done everything together, and suddenly we were told we couldn't even be in the same classes or have the same friends. I hated it. All because some stupid old Magics were sitting in their ivory tower dictating what we could and couldn't do."

Tray smiled and shook his head. "You sound so much like my younger sister Emily. She was always threatening to beat someone up for bullying us Nothings."

Oh Fates. I'd thought Tray was hot when I'd first met him, but when he smiled, butterflies started doing callisthenics in my stomach. *Stop it, Sarah. Molly's in there going through hell, and you're out here salivating over her... whatever. Some friend you are!*

I tore my eyes away from his and looked down at

the table. I needed to just make idle conversation. The problem was that I had no idea what we could even talk about. "So… can I ask how you learned that you were an Immune?"

"My dad had a magic shield set up around his workspace in the basement." Tray shrugged and frowned down at his hands. I immediately wanted to kick myself for making his gorgeous smile disappear. "I went to get him for dinner and walked straight through the damn thing."

"At least you were lucky it didn't happen in public."

Tray nodded, then sighed. "Yeah, it was way less traumatic than what Molly went through. But it still tore my family apart. Mum was convinced it was all her fault that I was both a Nothing and an Immune. No matter what Dad and I said, nothing would convince her otherwise. But at least Dad had been in a good position to keep it quiet and make arrangements for us to leave before anyone found out.

I reached out and squeezed Tray's hand. "I'm so sorry you all had to go through that. It's not fair how this stupid system tears families apart."

Tray looked down at their joined hands, then back up into her eyes. "Thanks for listening. It's great to talk to someone who understands what we've all been through."

We sat in comfortable silence for a while, each lost in our own thoughts. I was about to ask another question when we heard a commotion coming from my tent.

Tray jumped to his feet, his eyes wide with concern. "Molly!"

Which was when I realised I was still holding Tray's hand.

Tray

I DROPPED Sarah's hand and raced towards the tent. What the hell had I been thinking, sitting there holding hands with Sarah while Molly was going through hell? Guilt washed over me as I burst through the tent flap, ready to rescue Molly from her nightmare.

I froze in the doorway, my mind fighting to accept the level of intimacy portrayed in the scene before me. Sam sat on the floor with Molly curled up in his lap, her face buried against his chest. His arms were wrapped protectively around her as he stroked her hair while whispering in her ear in a calm, soothing tone. Bloody hell. Where was the hard-as-nails, gravelly-voiced guy who'd brought us here? Body-swapped apparently.

"Ummm... is everything okay?" I asked, my chest

tightening as I tried to keep the concern out of my voice.

Sam looked up, his eyes wary. "Yeah, we're good. Just had to deal with a slight panic attack, but she's calmed back down now."

Molly lifted her head from Sam's chest at the sound of my voice. My heart twisted at the sight of her red, puffy eyes, but she managed a weak smile. "I'm okay, Tray. Sam's been helping me work through some breathing exercises."

I nodded, trying to hide my worry that she wanted to stay in Sam's arms. "That's good. Do you need anything? Water? A snack?"

"No, I'm fine," Molly said softly. "I think I just need some time to rest and process everything."

Sam looked at me, and I thought I saw a hint of apology in his eyes. "Maybe it's best if we give her some space for a bit. I can stay with her if you want to go get some air."

Part of me wanted to insist on staying, but I could see Molly was still shaken. If Sam was helping her to stay calm, I didn't want to be the one responsible for setting her off again. Damn, that sounded selfish, even to my own ears. But hadn't I already caused her enough pain? If Sam could help her better than me, then who was I to stand in the way?

Reluctantly, I nodded. "Okay. I'll be right outside if you need me, Molly."

I stepped back out of the tent, my mind swirling with conflicting emotions. On one hand, I was glad Molly was getting help to work through her panic attack. But the sight of her wrapped in Sam's arms seriously made my skin itch. Although Sam was proving to be nothing like the riff-raff I'd labelled him at our first meeting.

Sarah was waiting when I came out of the tent, her beautiful face marred by worry. "Is Molly okay?"

I sighed and tried to feign relief. "Yeah, I think so. Sam's helping her with some breathing exercises. He said it seems to be calming her down."

Sarah nodded and smiled. "Oh, that's great news. Though I'm not really surprised. I told you Sam was good at this kind of thing. You don't need to worry. Sam will take good care of her."

"Yeah," I muttered, trying to hide my frustration. "That's not exactly making me feel any better."

Sarah raised an eyebrow, tilting her head as if studying me. "And why do you think that might be?"

I immediately wanted to kick myself for saying too much. "Forget I said anything. I'm just worried about Molly, that's all."

Sarah continued to study me, understanding in those beautiful hazel eyes. "Okay… so you're worried she might fall for Sam while he's helping her, and *you* have feelings for her. Am I close?"

Damnit. I wanted to tell Sarah that my feelings for

Molly weren't like that. But I wasn't ready for Sam to know he had no competition.

"Hey, it's okay. I get it. I loved Molly from the minute I met her, too. But carrying on like a jealous idiot isn't going to help anyone. What she needs right now is a friend."

"Fine, I know you're right. I need to stop being such a selfish jerk. This needs to be all about Molly."

"Awesome. I'm so glad we agree." Sarah's smile was breathtaking as she looked up into my eyes. "So, now that's sorted, how about we grab a fresh coffee and talk for a while? It might even help to take your mind off things."

I nodded, a sheepish smile creeping across my face. "Yeah, that sounds great. Thanks, Sarah."

We walked back to where we'd been sitting earlier in a comfortable silence, grabbing a fresh coffee and sitting down together.

"So, I'd love to know more about your sister, Emily. You said I remind you of her?" Sarah asked.

It felt good to talk about my family. Sarah listened with what appeared to be genuine interest, asking questions and sharing her own stories. Before we knew it, an hour had passed, and we both agreed we needed another coffee, and maybe something to eat.

As we moved to where the coffee and food supplies were laid out, I noticed a few people giving us curious looks. Okay, I knew what it must look like. I'd arrived with Molly and was now getting cosy with Sarah. But nothing like that was going on. Sarah was just trying to be a supportive friend.

Even if I did wish there was more...

CHAPTER SIXTEEN

Sam

I was determined not to stop the calming exercises until I was sure Molly's breathing had steadied. *Yep, it had nothing to do with wanting to prolong her position on my lap and in my arms.* "How are you feeling now?" I asked gently.

"Better," Molly replied. "Thank you so much for helping me through that."

Molly shifted in my lap, and I reluctantly loosened my hold on her. As much as I wanted to keep her close, I knew she needed space.

"I'm glad I could help," I said softly. "Do you want to talk about what triggered the panic attack?"

She shook her head. "Not really, but I guess I should. I was doing okay until that chair hit the wall, and the dust started crumbling. I just...I felt so trapped.

Like the walls were closing in." She visibly shuddered at the memory.

"Yeah, I get that. It was the last thing you needed to happen when you were already struggling with being down here. But hopefully, that was an anomaly, and it won't happen again," I hesitated, then added, "We can take things slow. No one's going to force you to stay down here if you're not ready."

Molly looked up at me, her beautiful brown eyes searching mine. "Really? But I thought—"

"We're just trying to make you feel comfortable here, not traumatise you," I explained. "Keeping you here until you were calm and in control was part of the process. Unless you stayed and made your decision to leave calmly rather than bolt out of here in a panic, or wake up already back outside, you'd never have even considered coming back in."

Molly nodded, relief evident on her face. "Thank you, Sam. I really appreciate everything you've done." She paused, biting her lip. "I still feel pretty stupid, though. Everyone must think I'm a complete nutter."

I shook my head and smiled at her reference to herself. "No one thinks you're a nutter, Molly. I'm sure just about everyone here has had their own personal trauma and anxiety to deal with at some time in their lives. Even *before* discovering they were Immunes. Although, that, in itself, was a huge adjustment."

"Even for you?" she asked softly.

I hesitated, then nodded. "Yeah, even for me. It wasn't easy leaving everything behind."

Molly studied my face. "Do you want to talk about it?"

Part of me wanted to deflect, to keep my walls up like I usually did. But there was something about the open acceptance in Molly's eyes that made me want to tell her everything.

"To be honest, I turned into an angry Douchebag when I first discovered I was an Immune. Sarah had tried to cast an illusion on me for a fancy-dress party, and we couldn't understand why it wasn't working. You can imagine Mum and Dad's reaction when we told them what happened, or should I say *didn't* happen."

Molly nodded and then sighed. "I think I was too numb and shocked to even be angry. Not that I had time to feel much of anything. One minute, everything was fine, and the next, I was running for my life. There were actual witnesses when I was exposed."

"Yeah, I know I didn't have it as bad as lots of other people. But I was just so pissed off," I admitted. "I had my whole life planned out. I was all set to follow in my dad's footsteps and become a successful businessman. I had a girlfriend I planned to marry someday. Being an Immune shattered all of that in an instant. My entire future was ripped away, and I had no say in any of it."

Molly listened intently, her eyes full of empathy. So

much so that I found myself opening up more than I had in a long time.

"The hardest part was seeing the devastation in my parents' eyes. They tried to hide it, but I could tell they saw me differently after that. And, on top of that, my girlfriend, my childhood sweetheart no less, dropped me like a hotcake as soon as she found out." I tried to swallow the bitterness those memories evoked.

"But the best *and the worst* of it was when Sarah insisted she was *coming-on-the-run* with me." I shook my head. "While I was secretly relieved and excited that we wouldn't be apart, it felt like I was responsible for ruining her life too."

"That wasn't your fault," Molly said softly, reaching out to squeeze my hand. "Sarah made her own decision."

I sighed and nodded. "I know that… *logically.* But it's still hard not to feel guilty sometimes. Sarah gave up *everything* to come with me, and she chose to do it."

"She clearly loves you, Sam," Molly said. "Anyone can see how close the two of you are."

I smiled. "Yeah, we've always been really close. I don't know what I'd do without her. She's kinda my rock."

I was surprised by how easy it felt to open up to Molly. There was something about her that made me feel… well, comfortable, I guess. And that was something I'd only ever really felt with Sarah.

"Thank you for sharing that with me," Molly said. "It

helps to know I'm not the only one totally over-whelmed by all this."

"You're definitely not alone in that," I assured her. "All those people out there are in exactly the same boat as us."

Molly's eyes met and held mine for no more than a few heartbeats. I tried to ignore the weird feeling in my chest, the one increasing my heartbeat and making me feel lightheaded.

Oh, and speaking of boats, mine was so far up shit creek without a paddle that it was ridiculous.

Molly

GAZING into Sam's clear hazel eyes, the level of warmth and understanding radiating from their depths made my heart flutter and my stomach twist. All my earlier fears and anxieties melted away into the stratosphere.

Until reality came crashing back in. *Good grief, Molly. What the hell are you doing?* I was still under-ground, still an Immune on the run, and Tray was waiting for me outside. Waves of guilt washed over me as I remembered how supportive Tray had been through everything.

"I should probably go check on Tray," I said softly, breaking eye contact. "He must be worried."

Sam nodded, and I might have imagined the flicker of disappointment in his eyes before he masked it. "Of course. So, you feel ready to go back out there?"

I took a deep breath, steeling myself. "I think so. Thanks to you."

Sam helped me to my feet, keeping a steadying hand on my elbow as we exited the tent. I covered my eyes for a second as they adjusted to the brighter light of the main cavern. I tried to ignore the rocky walls surrounding us on all sides, my rapid heartbeat telling me it wasn't working. Okay, maybe a new tactic was needed. Calling up the breathing techniques Sam had taught me, it didn't take long for it to settle back into its normal rhythm.

I scanned the area for Tray, finally spotting him sitting with Sarah at one of the tables. They looked deep in conversation, laughing together about something. I quickly squashed the pang of jealousy that shot through me. Hell, it didn't look anywhere near as bad as the intimate moment I'd just shared with Sam. I had no right to feel possessive of Tray.

As we approached, Tray looked up, and his face broke into a relieved smile. "Molly! Feeling better?"

"Much," I said, managing a small smile. "In fact, I could really go for one of those sandwiches and a coffee right now."

Tray went to jump up, but Sam put his hand on his

arm. "Maybe you should sit here with Molly, and I'll grab the sustenance. To be honest, I could do with some myself."

Tray threw him a grateful look, and they both nodded. Aargghh… sometimes being around these two men was like dealing with a couple of cavemen. *Well, at least they should feel right at home where we are right now.* I tried to stifle the giggle rising up my throat.

"Hey, what's so funny? What'd I miss?" Sarah asked from the other side of where Tray sat.

"Let's just say, *Ugh, men hunt* and leave it at that," I said with a wink.

Sarah and I both cracked up laughing while Tray just scratched his head in confusion. Hot damn, it felt good to laugh. Life had become way too serious lately. Sarah had been right about one thing. The cavern was so open and huge it was easy to forget where we were. Unless, of course, some idiot decided to throw something against the wall and started the whole *here-comes-the-cave-in* thing again.

Sam placed a sandwich and a coffee in front of me and then slid onto the bench seat beside me. "So, from the raucous laughter coming from over here a minute ago, I'm assuming I missed something big?"

"Don't ask," Tray said, rolling his eyes. "Apparently, it was a girl thing." At which Sarah and I busted up all over again.

I tried to quell the laughter so I could devour the ham and cheese sandwich Sam had given me. I couldn't remember the last time I'd eaten. As I quickly devoured the one I had, I was already wondering whether I could convince Sam to make me another one. But before I could even ask, Sam had pushed his sandwich over in front of me and mouthed *enjoy*.

I was about to object when he held up his hand, shook his head and got up to make himself another one. *Wow... spoiled much?* I sat back and sipped my coffee, finally relaxing for the first time in days. Maybe I could do this after all.

Sam was just slipping back onto the bench seat when a deafening boom echoed through the cavern, shaking dust and pebbles loose from the ceiling. Shouts of fear and panic erupted as everyone scrambled for cover.

"They've found us. We're being attacked!" Sam yelled, grabbing my arm and pulling me toward a more sheltered area.

My heart raced as flashes of magical energy blasted against the holographic entrance. Panic threatened to overwhelm me again, but I forced myself to take deep breaths. No way I could lose it now.

Chaos erupted around us as Immunes ran in all directions, grabbing weapons and taking up defensive positions. Sam pushed me behind him protectively as he drew a gun from his waistband.

Sarah appeared at my elbow as if out of nowhere. "There's a secret back exit we need to get to. My magical hologram won't last through much more of their onslaught. Either that or they'll blast their way in somewhere else."

Wait. The Magics were attacking the walls, which were inanimate objects. So, if I was touching the wall when it hit, could I just…?

Determined not to let the panic win yet again, I raced toward the wall closest to the stairs. I held my breath as I reached out to touch it, praying it worked the same way the car had.

The wall shuddered slightly, and my knees almost buckled at the magic pouring out of the walls and flooding into my body. The usual tingling sensation seemed to have morphed into debilitating tremors, and I felt ready to explode.

And then I breathed a sigh of relief as Tray appeared beside me, sliding an arm around my waist as I sagged against him. "Have you got it? The magic?" he whispered in my ear.

I nodded and ground out the words. "There's too much. Help me."

"Okay, sweetheart. We're gonna get rid of it just like last time. Do you think you can do the *return-to-sender* thing again?"

"Can't lift my arms," I muttered, and Tray knew at once what I meant. He lifted the hand that had touched the wall, and I wiggled my fingers, pushing the magic out like I'd done before. I clung to Tray as we both flew backwards from the impetus needed to release the magic.

Another deafening boom rocked the cavern, but this time it sounded like it came from outside. A shocked silence filled the air, only to be shattered by the screams of agony that were definitely coming from outside.

Tray sat us both up, his arms wrapped around me as we waited for the uncontrollable shaking wracking my body to stop. When I felt sure the last of the excess magic had drained from my system, the shaking stopped, and I slumped against Tray in relief.

"What the hell just happened?" Sam demanded, racing over with Sarah close behind him.

Tray looked up at them, his eyes wide with a mixture of awe and fear. "Molly absorbed the magic from their attacks through the wall and sent it back at them."

Sam's jaw dropped as he stared at Molly. "That's...that's impossible. How? No wait. There'll be time for explanations later. Right now, someone needs to go up to the surface and see what happened."

He waved Tom and Mike over, then turned to head up the stairs.

"Now just hang on a minute. Don't you think it would be wise to take a Magic up there with you?" Sarah chirped, moving up to stand beside Sam. "Cause regardless, I'm coming too."

Tray helped me to my feet, his arm still wrapped protectively around my waist. I leaned heavily against him, my legs shaky and my head spinning from the massive surge of magic that had coursed through my body.

"And so am I. So don't bother arguing with *me* either." Sam just rolled his eyes and walked back to help Tray.

Supported between Sam and Tray, we made our way up the stairs, my heart pounding harder with each step. What would we find on the surface? Had I really managed to repel an entire squad of attacking Magics?

But nothing could have prepared us for what we found. We all just froze in shock as we emerged into the harsh sunlight, horrified by the carnage before us.

A massive crater, easily 50 metres across and just as deep, had opened up in the dusty earth where, moments ago, there had been solid ground. The edges were scorched black, still smoking from the intense magical blast. Bits of twisted metal and shattered magical artifacts were scattered everywhere.

But it was the sight of the ravaged bodies that made my stomach lurch. Scattered around the rim and tumbled into the pit itself were the unconscious—or possibly dead—bodies of dozens of Magics and Councillors.

Their robes were tattered and singed, limbs splayed at unnatural angles. A few twitched or groaned weakly, but most lay ominously still. The air reeked of ozone and burnt flesh.

Sam and Tray caught me as my knees gave out yet again, somehow managing to hold me steady between them. The acrid stench of smoke and charred flesh filled the air, making us all gag.

"Dear Fates," Sarah whispered, her face pale as she surveyed the devastation I'd caused. "How...? Why...?"

Sam took in the situation through wary eyes. Then he looked directly into mine. "This is exactly what they'd have done to us if given the chance. Now come on, we need to get outta here. I'm sure there'll be more of them on their way already, and we need to be a long way from here when they arrive."

CHAPTER SEVENTEEN

Sarah

The reality of our situation hit me like a punch to the gut. We had just taken out an entire squad of Magics and Councillors. There was no going back from this. We'd officially gone from *lab-rats-in- the-making* to *execute-on-sight!*

"Everyone, listen up!" Sam's voice boomed out, snapping us all to attention. "We don't have long before reinforcements will arrive. Only grab what you can carry, and meet at the emergency evacuation point in five minutes. Move!"

The cavern erupted into controlled chaos as people scrambled to gather whatever they could. Tents were hastily collapsed, backpacks stuffed with food and supplies. Children cried as parents scooped them up. The air filled with a cacophony of urgent whispers and shuffling feet. The cavern that had been our home for so long now buzzed with nervous energy as everyone prepared to flee.

But what bothered me the most, was that no-one seemed ready or able to address our biggest issue. We knew we couldn't stay here, but where the hell could we possibly go?

I cursed at my shaking hands as I worked to shove clothes and supplies into my backpack. To be honest, I was struggling with the enormity of everything that had just happened to the point where I was close to losing it. We'd been discovered. Our safe haven was compromised. And Molly had somehow unleashed a devastating magical attack that had wreaked death and destruction on a level I'd never seen before. So how the hell was that even possible for someone who supposedly had no magic? Maybe there was more to Molly than any of them knew.

Pushing the thoughts aside for a time when I could get some answers, I was just grabbing the last of my stuff from my tent, when my fingers brushed against something hard in the pocket of the jacket I'd worn the previous day. *Bloody hell.* It was Tray's dad's phone. In all the chaos, I'd completely forgotten I still had it.

Just then, as if on cue, the phone began to vibrate. My heart almost leapt into my throat as I pulled it out and saw "Dad" flashing on the screen. With trembling fingers, I answered the call.

"Hello?" I whispered, my voice hoarse and scratchy.

"Molly?" Tray's Dad sounded frantic.

"No, this is Sarah. I'm Sam's sister."

"Sarah? Thank Fates. I've been trying to reach you. Are you all okay? What happened?" fear and worry crackled in Tray's dad's voice.

"We're alive, but there was an attack. Molly...she did something impossible. Reflected their magic back at them somehow. The Magics and the Councillors. They're... they're all dead."

I heard the sharp intake of breath, and I had to keep swallowing to hold back the sobs. "Hello? Are you still there?" I finally asked.

"Fates preserve us," the older man breathed, his voice a blend of horror and relief. "I can't believe... but you're all okay? Tray and Molly too?"

"Yep, we're all alive," I said quickly. "But we have to leave like right now. We're expecting the Council's reinforcements to arrive any minute. Not that anybody seems to have a clue about where we should go from here."

There was a pause, filled only by the sound of the older man's ragged breathing. When he spoke again, his voice was low and urgent.

"Listen carefully, Sarah. There may be a place you can go. I've heard whispers, rumours really, of a hidden sanctuary for Immunes and those rare Magics who are either bonded to them or who protect them. A place that the Council's magic can't penetrate."

My heart leapt. "Where? How do we find it?"

"It's called Zion. Supposedly it's somewhere in the Glass House Mountains, hidden deep in the forest. The stories say it's protected by powerful wards that block all magic. Even tracking spells don't work once you're inside their compound."

My mind was racing as I tried to absorb the information Tray's dad had shared. A hidden sanctuary, protected from magic? It sounded almost too good to be true. But we were so out of options.

Quickly thanking the man, I promised to have someone monitor the phone from now on and ended the call. And then I was racing to find Sam. I found him helping load supplies into our few remaining vehicles, barking orders and trying to quell the panic and mayhem.

"Sam!" I called out, grabbing his arm. "I need to speak to you. *Urgently.*" I knew I was babbling, but I thought it best I tell him about my news in private. Dragging him to where I hoped we'd be out of earshot, I sucked in a breath and spilled my guts, so to speak. "Okay, so I just got a call from Tray's dad. Remember he gave us that phone? Anyway, he was checking we were all okay, and when I told him we had to evacuate, he told me about a place we might be able to go."

Sam's eyes widened. "What? Where?"

I lowered my voice, not wanting to be overheard. "It's called Zion. Supposedly it's a sanctuary for Immunes hidden somewhere in the Glass House

Mountains, protected by powerful wards that block all magic. No one can so much as track us there."

"Okay, we need to tell Tray and Molly," Sam said urgently. "If this Zion place is real, it might be our only chance."

We pushed through the frantic crowd, scanning faces for our friends. Finally, Sam spotted Tray's tall form near one of the vehicles, helping Molly inside.

"Tray! Molly!" Sam called out as we jogged toward where Tray still stood. I hadn't seen Molly since we'd gone back into the cavern to pack up our things and she'd stayed up here with Tray. She hadn't been looking real good the last time I'd seen her, and I hoped she was recovered and feeling better soon.

Tray

I HELPED Molly into the back of the familiar beat-up van we'd used to get here the day before. At least all our stuff was still in here, so we didn't need to enter that cavern ever again. My heart ached at how pale and shaky Molly still looked. The magical backlash had taken a serious toll on her. I was about to climb in beside her when I heard Sam calling our names.

"Tray! Molly!" I turned to see Sam and Sarah jogging towards us, matching expressions of urgency on their faces. "We might finally have some good news," Sam said as they reached us, slightly out of breath.

I raised an eyebrow doubtfully. Good news had been in very short supply lately. "Oh?"

Sarah nodded eagerly. "I just got a call from your dad. He told me about a place we might be able to go. A sanctuary for Immunes."

Wow. I'd totally forgotten we still had Dad's phone. I smiled at the thought that Dad had come through yet again. "Hey, you don't have to convince me. Right now, my only goal is to be anywhere but here."

Sam nodded. "Yeah, I'm with you on that one. So, we need to get to the Emergency Evacuation Point in the next two minutes. I'll announce our plans and invite any who are interested to meet us there in a couple of days."

As soon as Sam and Sarah had grabbed their stuff, and we'd all piled into the van, Sarah drove us to the Emergency Evacuation Point. Sam jumped out and vaulted up onto the back of a nearby Ute so he could be heard. Taking a deep breath, he scanned the anxious faces around him and began.

"Okay people, you need to listen!" Sam's calm and steady words seemed to soothe some of the chaos. "We've found what we hope will be our new home. It's in the Glass House Mountains."

Confused looks and murmurs rippled through the group.

"Yeah, yeah... I know it probably sounds crazy," Sam continued, using his hands in a calming motion to cease the murmuring "But the intel we've received is from a reliable source, revealing the fact that a hidden sanctuary called Zion is there."

The crowd had become deathly quiet as they gave Sam their undivided attention. Sam swallowed and kept going.

"It's said to be protected by powerful wards that block all magic and make it impossible for even the best trackers to locate someone inside the wards. Unfortunately, we can't confirm the intel with the limited time we have to get out of here, but I believe this is our only option."

He paused again, as if giving them time for the information to sink in. When the murmurs had again died down, Sam ran his hand through his hair and looked around the small crowd. "I'm not gonna lie to you—nothing will be easy from here. The Glass House Mountains are rugged terrain, full of dense rainforest and steep volcanic peaks. We'll have to leave our vehicles eventually and continue on foot, with no idea what's ahead of us. It will test us all to our limits."

Sam's eyes blazed with determination. "For anyone who wants to join us, we are planning to meet in one of the towns somewhere close to one of the mountains' entrances. I need to do some research before I can go into any details. As soon as I've got more answers, I'll send the details via the usual channels."

"For those of you who don't plan on joining us on this crazy expedition, please try to stay safe until hopefully one day we can meet again under better circumstances." No one said a word as we all took in the ramifications of where our choices would lead us.

"Okay, time to go. Please remember to take different routes out of here and do not stay with more than one other vehicle. If you plan to travel together, try to arrange your next meeting point somewhere obscure every time you stop. Good luck and stay safe… all of you."

Sam stepped down from the back of the Ute. Though I wasn't the guy's biggest fan, I had to admit I felt sorry for him. From what I could tell, he'd created this home for the Immunes himself a couple of years ago and pretty much taken on the role of saviour, provider and protector. Losing everything he'd worked so hard to establish had to be a crushing blow. He looked both physically and emotionally shattered.

Okay, so maybe it was time I put aside our false rivalry—or at least where I was concerned—and offered Sam whatever help he needed. He was basically a good guy, and in different circumstances, we might have ended up as friends. Hey, who knew what the future had in store for any of us? We might *still* end up friends. Stranger things had been known to happen… every damn day.

CHAPTER EIGHTEEN

Molly

As I slowly drifted back to consciousness, I became aware of a warm, solid presence beneath my cheek. Blinking my eyes open, I realised that I was curled up against a sleeping Sam's chest, his arm draped protectively around me. Heat rushed to my face as I carefully extricated myself, trying not to wake him.

"Hey there, sleepyhead," Tray's voice came from the front seat. I looked up to see him watching me in the rearview mirror, a mix of relief and something else I couldn't quite identify in his eyes.

"How long was I out?" I asked groggily, running a hand through my tangled hair.

"About five hours," Tray answered, his eyes again

meeting mine briefly in the rearview mirror before returning to the road. "How are you feeling?"

I took stock of my body, surprised to find the bone-deep exhaustion from earlier had faded to a dull ache. "Better, I think. Still tired, but nothing like before."

Sarah twisted around in the passenger seat to face me, her eyes bright with concern. "We were pretty worried about you. That was some serious magic you channelled back there."

The events from earlier came rushing back—the attack, the overwhelming surge of power, the devastating aftermath. I shuddered, remembering the horrific scene we'd left behind. "Did I really...are they all...?"

"Dead? Yeah, most likely," Tray said grimly. "But it was self-defence, Molly. They would have killed us all if you hadn't stopped them."

I knew he was right, but I was still struggling to get my head around the fact that I'd killed all those people. I glanced out the window, trying to distract my thoughts away from the devastating events, and took in the unfamiliar landscape rushing by. The arid desert we'd left behind had given way to gently rolling hills covered in eucalyptus trees, their leaves shimmering silver-green in the late afternoon sunlight.

"Where are we?" I asked, my voice still rough with sleep.

"We're about an hour outside of Gympie." Sarah

supplied. "We've been driving for most of the day, taking backroads to avoid any major towns or cities."

I blinked, trying to process Sarah's words. Gympie? That was hundreds of kilometres from where we'd been. As I glanced around the van, taking in Tray's tense posture as he drove and Sarah's worried eyes watching me, I realised I was pretty much out of the loop completely thanks to my overly long nap.

"Okaaay… so I obviously missed quite a bit while I was out. Why are we heading for Gympie? Or rather what's in Gympie I should know about?"

Just then, Sam stirred beside me. He blinked a couple of times before his gaze settled on me. "Glad to see you're awake and ready to get back in the game," he said, a relieved smile spreading across his face. "So, you're feeling better?"

"Better, but very confused," I admitted. "I was just asking for an update on, well, everything."

Sam sat up and looked at Sarah. "Maybe you'd be the best one to continue filling Molly in? From what I've heard, you've been doing a pretty good job so far."

"Excuse me? Just how long have you been awake?" I asked, almost swooning at his cheeky grin.

"Oh, not long. Only since about the time I lost the nice comfy pillow I was snuggled up with."

Tray kept his eyes on the winding country road ahead, but I could see him glancing at me in the rearview mirror every so often, his brow furrowed with concern.

Sarah wriggled around, trying to get more comfortable as she twisted to face us. She was obviously busting to fill me in on everything I'd missed while unconscious.

"So, after you passed out," Sarah began, "we had to make some really quick decisions. Remember how we had Tray's dad's phone? Well, it rang just as I was finishing packing up my stuff. To make a long story short, his dad told me about a place he'd heard rumours about called Zion. Apparently, it's a haven for Immunes and those who protect them. Completely impervious to magic and tracking."

Sarah paused to take a breath and guzzle some water, and I sat staring at her, totally gobsmacked. We had somewhere safe to go? And it might not even be underground? This day was improving at a rate of knots!

"Anyway, Sam announced the plan to head for this Zion, which is somewhere in the Glass House Mountains. But we knew we couldn't all travel together—it might draw too much attention. So, we split up into smaller groups, each taking different routes." She looked at Sam sadly and he nodded. "We're not actually sure how many will decide to join us. We won't know until we get to the arranged meeting place."

I looked over at Sam, who sat stiffly with his head down, and my heart went out to him. He'd done so much to help us all, and I was sure he'd be gutted by the loss of those who chose to go elsewhere. I put my hand on his arm and squeezed. When he looked up, I smiled. "We all have to make our own choices in this life, remember? They'll all make their choices based on what they believe is best for them and their loved ones."

Sam looked at Sarah and then at me with understanding and gratitude. At least he seemed a little less lost after my words.

"Hey, I'm not finished yet. I haven't even told you why we're heading for Gympie . Basically, we decided to head further north first," Sarah continued. "Hopefully it will throw off anyone who might be tracking us. The plan is to circle back around to the Glass House Mountains tomorrow. We were planning to stop in Gympie tonight, if you're okay with that?"

I shrugged. "Fine with me. I'm just happy to be away from the mess we left behind. That was just… I mean… how could I?" I tried to stop the tears welling in my eyes from falling, but I knew I was fighting a losing battle. The images of the horror I'd caused seemed to be on a continuous loop, replaying over and over in my head.

Sam reached over and pulled me back into his arms. "Hey, it's completely normal to feel traumatised after everything that's happened. Especially when you'd only just started to recover from the other panic attack. But what you need to remember is that you didn't kill those people. You don't even have magic. All you did was send their own magic back at them, the magic *they* were using to try and kill *us*. Oh, and while we're on the subject, whatever you did back there should have been totally impossible. In fact, I'm pretty sure no one has ever even heard of anyone being able to do... well... that."

"Yep, that's exactly what I told her the first time it happened," Tray said, his face a mask as he watched Sam's arms stay wrapped around me as he drove.

Sam looked stunned. "Wait, so you've done that before? When? What happened? Why didn't you say anything about it?"

Damnit, I so didn't have it in me to explain what had happened. I'd already soaked poor Sam's shirt for the second time in one day, and I wanted to just keep my face buried against his chest. But I knew Sam and Sarah deserved some answers, so I lifted my head and threw Tray a pleading look. "Tray... please..."

Tray

WHEN MOLLY HAD STARTED to cry, and Sam pulled her into his arms, I'd wanted to slam on the brakes, get out of the car, pull *Sam* out of the car, and hold Molly for as long as she'd let me. But when I saw the imploring look in her eyes—when Sam wanted answers about the other time she'd reflected the magic back—I sighed and knew I'd have to step up.

I took a deep breath, knowing I had to explain everything carefully. I could feel the weight of Sam and Sarah's expectant gazes, even as I kept my eyes on the winding road ahead. These people had risked everything to help us—they deserved the truth.

"All right, I'll tell you what happened," I began, keeping my eyes on the winding road ahead. "It was the day after Molly found out she was an Immune, the day we left Medulla. We'd been on the road for a while when we both got that tingly feeling I've always associated with someone trying to use magic on me. We were both totally confused, until I noticed the car behind us had sped up, and they were gaining on us fast. Seriously, I was convinced we were screwed. Now that they'd confirmed for sure that we were Immunes, I knew they'd use their magic to try to disable the car next."

I paused, remembering the fear and adrenaline of that moment. The dusty road stretching endlessly before us, the sight of the ominous vehicle gaining ground reflected in the rearview mirror.

Shaking myself mentally out of the remembered fear, I glanced up into the rearview mirror, seeing Molly's tear-stained face looking up at me gratefully. I gave her a small nod before continuing. I knew Sam and Sarah were listening intently by the complete silence in the car.

"Things were looking pretty grim, and that's when it happened. *Molly's Miracle*, I called it. I'd put my foot flat to the floor, and Molly was gripping the dashboard utterly terrified—"

"Okay," Molly said, sitting up and appearing to shake off the earlier horror and lethargy. "Thank you so much for stepping up for me Tray, but I think I might need to explain it from here. It's kinda hard to describe how someone else was feeling." She smiled gratefully at me, and I returned the smile with a nod. I was so proud of her for rallying against the despair she'd almost given in to.

"So… as Tray said, I was gripping the dashboard pretty hard when the car kind of shuddered under my hands, and a tingling sensation ran up both of my arms. It was more intense than the usual tingly feeling when someone tried to use magic on you personally. And it didn't go away straight away either. No way! I held my breath, waiting for the engine to die or a tyre to blow, but the car was totally unaffected. Tray reckoned I'd made the car Immune by being in contact when the magic hit, and the shudder was the car's equivalent of the tingles we get when the magic didn't work."

CHAPTER NINETEEN

Molly

Sam squeezed my shoulder and grabbed a bottle of water from beside him. Opening the bottle, he handed it to me with a smile, and I guzzled it greedily. I'd been parched, and Sam just seemed to always know what I needed and when. "Thanks, Sam. I *so* needed that." I said with a grateful smile.

"Thought you might. Okay, so you were up to the best part. Ready to keep going?" he asked softly.

I nodded and sucked in a breath. "Okay, so as I'm sure you can imagine, I was pretty close to losing it at the thought of being an even bigger freak than a *normal* Immune—like *we* would *ever* be considered normal. Anyway, it was also starting to worry me that the tingling sensation was still running up and down my arms. Usually, the sensation would be gone by now."

"Meanwhile, Tray was hooting and laughing about how amazing I was, and how the only thing that could make it even better would be if we could do something to disable their car. Which was when *the* most ridiculous thought I'd ever had started running through my mind. I looked down at my still-tingling hands, wondering why it hadn't stopped. Then, realising *everything* that had happened in the last twenty-four hours should have been ridiculous, I decided to give the crazy idea a go."

"So I just turned, pointed at the Councillors' car, kind of aimed my fingers and tried to push the tingling out of the ends of them. I heard the tyres of the other car blow at the exact same time the tingling stopped. I just sat in my seat like a stunned mullet as the other car crashed, totally disabled."

Tray was now laughing and hitting the steering wheel just like when I'd actually done the... *thing*. "You should have seen it, guys. It was absolutely amazing. No wait, *she* was absolutely amazing."

"But it was different that time," I said, my voice getting raspier from talking. "With the car, it was just a small amount of magic—probably from one Mage trying to stop us. The tingling was just like static electricity, and then I pushed it back out. It was gone pretty much instantly, and I was fine afterwards. Maybe a little tired, but nothing major."

I paused, taking a shuddering breath. "But at the cavern... it was more like being hit by a tsunami of energy. I could barely contain it, let alone control it. You have no idea. Then, when I started to push it back out, it felt like my blood was on fire. And it seemed to take forever to get it all out."

Sam leaned forward, his eyes wide. "Molly, this is all just so incredible. I've never heard of anything like it."

Tray nodded, finally coming back down off his high from the memories. "Neither had we. We were both pretty freaked out by it, to be honest. So now you know why we didn't share what happened with people we'd known for like five minutes."

"But I was *fine* afterwards," I stressed again, my voice now getting a bit shaky. "It was such a small amount of magic compared to..." She trailed off, her entire body shuddering.

"Compared to what happened at the cavern," Tray finished for me, still smiling into the rearview mirror. I threw him a grateful look.

Sam groaned. "From what you've said, it sounds like there may have been more than one Mage responsible for the blast you absorbed in the cavern. Think about it, you were touching the wall, which surrounded the entire cavern. They could have all been focused on the one spot and released their combined magic together. No wonder the devastation was so bad. Imagine the damage it would have done to the entire cavern if you hadn't stopped it. And *I* still can't believe taking in that much magic didn't kill you."

Sam

NO ONE SPOKE for a while after that, everyone seemingly lost in their own thoughts, no doubt trying to digest everything we'd just heard. I couldn't stop my mind from replaying the events at the cavern over and over. The deafening boom, the panic, and then Molly...

Oh, dear Fates... Molly. My stomach churned as I thought about just how close we'd come to losing her. How the hell had her body been able to take in that much raw magical energy? I couldn't rid myself of the thought that what she'd done should have killed her instantly. That she was alive was nothing short of a miracle.

She looked so fragile, yet I knew better now. Studying her pale face and the dark circles under her eyes, I was mesmerised by her presence. This girl was more powerful than anyone I'd ever encountered. In fact, she held a power that could change everything. Were there others like her out there we didn't know about?

All that aside, the other thing that continued to amaze me, was how Molly had managed to burrow so deeply under *my* skin in such a short time. I'd spent years carefully guarding my heart, determined never to let anyone get close enough to hurt me again. But Molly had somehow slipped past all my defences without even trying.

As I gazed down at her, I was once again stunned by how beautiful she was. Her long lashes fanned across her cheeks, still damp with tears. A few strands of her chestnut hair had escaped from her messy ponytail, curling softly around her face.

"We're five kilometres out of Gympie. Any ideas about where we can stay?" I was snapped out of my thoughts by Tray's almost growling voice coming from the front.

I tore my eyes away from Molly, feeling a mix of guilt and frustration. I knew Tray had feelings for her too—it was obvious in every protective glance, every concerned frown. And here I was, holding her in my arms, staring at her like some lovesick puppy. I seriously needed to get my head out of my butt and back in the game.

"Ooh, I have an idea," Sarah said, trying to act nonchalant to cover the excitement in her voice. "If anyone's interested, I *may* have found somewhere good to stay for the night."

"Oh yeah? I don't know about the others, but I'm definitely interested. What you got?" Not that I was surprised. Sarah had always been good at finding what others couldn't, often in the most bizarre places.

Sarah's fingers flew across her phone screen as she pulled up the details. "It's this old homestead about fifteen minutes the other side of town. Apparently, it used to be a working farm, but now they rent out some of the outbuildings as holiday cottages. It's secluded, off the main road, and they take cash payments."

I nodded approvingly. Cash was good. We'd just sign in under fake names. I always carried a couple of false ID cards. The last thing we needed to do was leave any kind of paper trail.

"Okay Little Miss Navigator. I'm ready for directions to this amazing five-star accommodation," Tray said, as Sarah held up her hand for a High Five and Tray grinned as he complied.

Holy shit! Tray had almost sounded jovial. Wonders would never cease.

CHAPTER TWENTY

Sarah

As we pulled into the long, dusty driveway meandering toward the homestead, I couldn't help but steal one last glance at Tray's profile. Somehow, he managed to look more gorgeous every time I looked at him. My heart did a little flip as he caught me looking, flashing me a quick smile before returning his focus to navigating what could no longer be called a road.

Somehow, being this close together in a car for five hours had changed everything. Or maybe it was just *my* perception that had shifted. Either way, I was in serious trouble.

At first, I'd just been impressed by how calmly he handled the stress of our hasty escape. I'd been a bundle of nerves, while Tray exuded an oddly reassuring calmness. Actually, I'd spent the entire drive sneaking glances at him, hanging on his every word as we chatted about everything and nothing. I loved the way his eyes crinkled when he laughed, the quiet strength in his voice as he recounted his and Molly's harrowing escape from Medulla.

A flutter of excitement raced through me at the view laid out before us as we approached the old homestead. The setting sun blanketed the sprawling property in a golden glow, somehow softening the view of weathered wooden fences and fields dotted with grazing cattle. The main house was a charming two-story Queenslander, its wide wraparound veranda inviting those who wanted to sit and watch the sunset.

But it was the collection of rustic cottages scattered across the property that really caught my attention. Each one looked unique—from the converted barn with its soaring ceilings, to the cosy log cabins nestled among the gum trees. But it was what looked to be the old sheep shearing shed, now transformed into quirky accommodation, that really got me excited. I would seriously love to stay in a place like that.

I pulled the boots I'd discarded hours ago back onto my feet, as Tray parked the van in the designated parking area, a short walk from the main house. I turned to share my excitement with Molly and Sam, closing my mouth as I noticed how protective Sam had become of Molly, practically lifting her out of the van. He kept one arm around her waist, steadying her when she wobbled slightly. The tender concern in his eyes as he gazed down at her made my breath catch.

I'd never seen my brother look at *anyone* that way before. Not even Rebecca and I'd been sure she was *the one* for him. But the way he looked at Molly... it was like she'd hung the moon and stars.

A tiny spark of hope ignited in my chest. If Sam was falling for Molly, did that mean I might actually have a chance with Tray? I'd been trying so hard to squash my growing feelings for him, convinced he only had eyes for Molly.

I mean, it was clear to anyone with eyes that Tray had feelings for Molly. I'd seen the way he looked at her, how fiercely protective he was. But the fact that Sam seemed to be edging into the picture didn't change Tray's feelings for Molly, or Molly's for him. Did it?

I'd been fighting my growing attraction to Tray all day, trying to convince my stupid heart it was foolish to develop feelings for a guy I barely knew. *Not* to mention that said guy wanted someone else, or that we were all way too busy trying to stay alive to worry about who was attracted to whom. But no matter how hard I tried to ignore it, there was just something about Tray that drew me to him like a moth to a flame.

As Tray stretched his tall frame after the long drive, I couldn't stop my eyes from tracing the lean lines of his amazing body. Was it any wonder Molly had fallen for him on sight? The guy was serious model material.

Wait. That thought had raised an interesting theory

in my admittedly slightly deranged brain. What if Molly and Tray's feelings had been strengthened by their *circumstances* rather than real romantic attraction? I mean honestly, they hadn't even kissed. Okay, so maybe they'd only met, what, just over a week ago. But I'd only known Tray a couple of days, and if he hadn't already shown his interest in Molly, I'm pretty sure I'd have cornered and kissed him way before now.

Right, so maybe it was time for me and Molly to have some serious girl-time, just the two of us. It felt like this stay in Gympie was offering a very much needed time-out from all the running-for-our-lives-from-people-trying-to-kill-us crap. Yep, we needed to take advantage of the short reprieve. Because if I didn't deal with this pining-for-the-wrong-guy crap soon, I wouldn't have to worry about those people trying to kill us, I seriously might just implode.

Tray

I CLIMBED out of the van, stretching my stiff muscles after the long drive. As I took in our surroundings—from the dilapidated but still functional wooden fences to the rustic cottages dotting the property—I felt a strange mix of relief and unease settle over me. We were safe for the moment, but for how long?

My eyes drifted to Molly as she was practically lifted out of the van by Sam, who kept an arm around her waist when she looked a bit wobbly. A whole new feeling twisted in my gut. Seeing them together no longer filled me with the same burning resentment it had before. Instead, I found myself envious of what they'd found. And I was actually starting to be okay with seeing them together.

Then I found my gaze drawn to Sarah as she emerged from the passenger seat. Her green eyes seemed to sparkle as she took in our surroundings, a smile playing on her lips. I didn't know how or why, but this girl actually made me breathless. And it wasn't just because of her outer beauty. It was more her constant state of happiness and the incredible resilience she exuded, such rare commodities in the dreary world I'd been trapped in for so long. She looked up and our eyes met, the warm smile she flashed me causing my heart to skip a beat.

I shook my head, shifting my gaze back to Molly, watching her lean heavily against Sam as they waited for Sarah and me to join them. That same pang of... something... twisted in my chest again. But I knew it was no use longing for Sarah and I to have what they had with each other. Sure, she was always pleasant when we were together. But an Immune and a Magic? *No way...*

I shook my head and walked around the car to join the others. I'd decided one thing was for sure. I needed to sort my head out while we had this temporary reprieve from all the bullshit that had become our lives. It was definitely time to talk to… well… someone.

Molly

BY THE TIME Sam had practically lifted me out of the van, keeping one arm firmly around my waist, I knew he was the one I wanted. What I had thought were strong feelings for Tray had withered to insignificance compared to what I felt for Sam. I knew I still needed Sam's physical support, my legs still felt shaky, and my body was still drained from the magical onslaught. But it wasn't just my physical weakness needing Sam's continuing presence.

I'd been so lost in a whirlwind of conflicting emotions since the day I met Tray and everything went haywire. Everything that had happened in the past week felt like snapshots from a lifetime ago, yet also as if they'd happened in the blink of an eye. My world had been turned upside down, and inside out. Everything I thought I knew about myself and my place in the world had been shattered into a million pieces.

And then there were the boys. Tray and Sam. Two totally handsome, kind, brave men who had both risked everything to keep me safe. I'd been so confused about my feelings for Tray when we first met. That instant spark, the way my heart raced whenever he smiled at me. It had felt like the beginning of something beautiful, something real. In those early days on the run, clinging to him had felt natural, even necessary. Tray had been my anchor in a storm of chaos and fear.

I had no doubt that the instant bond between us existed. But was it possible that the love I'd felt developing between us could be attributed to something closer to the deep affection of lifelong friends?

I glanced over at Tray, watching as he and Sarah fell into easy conversation, matching strides as they came over to join us. So where was the pang of jealousy I'd felt earlier? A week ago, I would have sworn I was falling in love with Tray.

But now, as I leaned against Sam's solid warmth, his arm protectively around my waist, I knew this was where I wanted to be. The way Sam looked at me as if I were the most important thing in his world, resonated with something deep within my soul.

But what about Tray's feelings? I could have sworn he only thought of me as another sister, until Sam and Sarah had come into our lives. Sarah had insisted that

Sam and Tray were both acting like rivals for my affections. And even I could see that my being with Sam upset Tray. What the hell was I supposed to do with that?

Thinking of Sarah gave me an idea. What if I asked for her advice, kind of like girl to girl? She seemed to have way more experience than me when it came to boys and friendships, and she'd known Sam their entire lives. Just thinking of talking to Sarah about all the emotional crap going on made me feel like the weight of the world that was currently perched on my shoulders had lightened just the tiniest bit.

CHAPTER TWENTY-ONE

Sam

By the time Tray and Sarah joined us, I'd formulated what our next move should be, surprised that Tray's eyes weren't throwing me the usual daggers for having my arm around Molly. Maybe he could see how much support she still needed just to be standing here, and had decided to back off with the whole jealousy thing?

"Okay", I said, looking mainly at Tray. "I was going to suggest you guys stay in the van, but I knew we all needed to get out and stretch our legs for a bit. But I think it would be best if Molly and Tray stay in the van while Sarah and I go check-in. And before anyone protests, you need to remember that Molly and Tray are wanted fugitives. Their photos will be everywhere, not to mention on every news channel."

Tray nodded, holding out a hand to Molly to help her back to the van. "You're right, Sam. Molly and I need to stay out of sight as much as possible. We'll be waiting for you in the van."

I gritted my teeth as Molly moved over to Tray's side, the other man's hand quick to replace mine at her waist. Sarah linked arms with me and turned me toward the house. "Come on bro, let's go do this so we can all relax and have a long overdue coffee."

I looked back over my shoulder to see Tray carefully helping Molly scramble back into the van. I knew she'd be fine, that Tray would keep her safe, but walking away, even for five minutes, was getting harder and harder to do.

"So whaddya think, should we see if the old shearers' shed is available so we can all stay together, or ask for two of the smaller cabins?" Sarah said, happily chirping along beside me.

"Definitely the large one where we can all be together. I don't like the idea of being separated if something happens," I said, trying not to sound like I cared all that much either way.

"Yep, I agree. Besides, it will give us all a chance to discuss what to expect when we get to the meet-up at Beerwah."

I just nodded in agreement as we knocked on a door with an *Office* sign on it. An elderly lady ushered us in the door, before closing it and heading for her chair behind the small desk.

"So, what can I do for you young'uns today?" She asked briskly, a smile on her wizened old face.

"We'd really like to stay in the old shearing shed if it's available?" Sarah piped up before I could open my mouth. "We have two other friends who are still in the van, she's been really carsick, and her boyfriend is looking after her. Would the shed be able to accommodate the four of us easily?"

Her smile became more sympathetic. "Oh dear, your poor friend. There's nothing worse than car sickness. But I've always found the best cure is to get out of the vehicle and rest for a while. Which is exactly what you're doing, good friends that you are."

She beamed and opened the journal on the desk in front of her. "Yes, I'm sure the shed would be best. There are a couple of lounges for you all to sit and drink coffee, the makings for which are all in the shed already. Now, do you need any food? I'm guessing you were unprepared for your unscheduled stop, so I have a few what I call *Survival Packages* on hand at all times. You'd be surprised how many people turn up here and are relieved to find they don't have to go back into town for food."

Sarah grinned and clapped her hands. "Oh, thank you so much. You are our saviour. Yes please, we'll take everything you think we'll need overnight for four people."

"Joe," the woman yelled towards a room at the back of the Office. "We need four *Survival Packages* out here right now. And don't even start with ya dawdlin' old man, these people need to get to the shearin' shed, yesterday."

She winked at Sarah and started to total the cost of our stay and food. I pulled out my wallet, sliding the false ID from its slot, but she just waved it away. "Put it away, son. We don't bother with details like that around here. Long as you're all paid up and don't destroy the place, then everybody's happy. Besides, us Nothings need to look after each other, cos those others sure won't."

I opened my mouth to ask how she'd known, and she just waved her hand. "I've been on this Earth for long enough to recognise a fellow Nothing, son."

Smiling at the old woman's words, I pulled out enough cash to cover what she'd asked for, plus a little bit extra to thank her for making us feel so welcome. Just then, an old man bustled in from the other room, pushing a trolley laden with four large packages.

"Where d' ya want 'em?" he asked, dragging his hat off so he could scratch his balding head.

"Hey, thanks Joe. We can probably handle it from here, and I'll bring the trolley right back," I offered, worried he might catch sight of Molly or Tray and recognise them.

Joe just grunted, pushed the trolley to me, and turned and left. Okay then—man of few words.

"Not much for conversation is my Joe. But he's a good man and that'll do me. Now, here's the key. Off you go and get that poor sick girl out of that vehicle. You know where to go?"

Sarah bounced excitedly on her feet. "Oh yes, we saw it on our way in. It looked so awesome, I can't wait to see it up close."

The old lady just chuckled and waved us goodbye. "Oh, and just remember," she called as we were almost out the door. "You should always be careful what you wish for, young'un."

Sarah

THE CLOSER WE got to the old shearing shed, the more the old woman's words started to make sense.

The old sheep shearing shed, now transformed into quirky accommodation, was a sight to behold. What appeared to be the original wooden beams and walls were still intact, but now there were colourful mismatched doors and windows added, making it look like a well-loved dollhouse. Moss and vines clung to the walls, giving it a natural, earthy feel.

As soon as we pulled up at what we assumed was a front door, I grabbed the key Sam had put in the centre console earlier and jumped from the van. Holding my breath as I opened the door, I sighed with relief at the welcome sight before me.

Although rough and weathered on the outside, the interior had been lovingly renovated with smooth, polished wood floors and soft, cosy furnishings. The entire area felt spacious and inviting.

The walls were adorned with soft tapestries and the furnishings were a mix of plush chairs and soft, fluffy blankets, all arranged in a way that created a sense of comfort and cosiness.

"Hurry up, you guys," I called over my shoulder. "You need to see this place. It's totally cool."

"Then how about you move out of the doorway so we can all get in," Sam said almost playfully. It had been a long time since I'd heard that tone in his voice, and whatever was causing it needed to stay right where it was. Unfortunately, I had a bad feeling that achieving that goal would be harder than it should have been.

Molly stood in the doorway with a huge smile on her face, looking less stressed than in the entire time I'd known her. Okay, so I may have only known her for a couple of days, but from what I'd learned about both her and Tray, I think it might have been the closest to stress-free we'd all been for quite some time.

"And you should be sitting down," Sam said, taking Molly's hand and leading her over to a plush two-seater lounge near the centre of the large space. "After all, we told the old lady that our friend stayed in the van because she was *so* carsick, and she said we had to take very good care of our poor friend." He chuckled as he settled Molly into the chair and then turned to the rest of us.

"Right, time to get all our crap in from the van. I'm dying to see what the old lady considered necessary to include in her *Survival Packages*."

I waited for the boys to head out to the van before I ran over to Molly and grabbed her hand. "Okay, I really need some one-on-one girl-talk at the first possible opportunity. You up for it?"

Molly grinned and squeezed my hand. "You must have read my mind. I need exactly the same thing. Hey, do we even know what the available sleeping arrangements are? I mean, this lounge is really comfy, but—"

"Sarah, get your butt out here and give us a hand. We all wanna stop for the day too, you know," Sam yelled from outside.

"Sorry, I'm coming now. I was just checking Molly didn't need anything," I replied. Funny how that seemed to be an acceptable excuse to both boys, cos neither bothered with a come-back.

Molly

DECIDING I didn't need the angst over who got to sit next to me on the lounge when the unpacking was finished, I pulled my legs up beside me and snuggled into the soft cushions.

I was excited about the girl talk Sarah and I had planned, and was determined to snatch up the first opportunity to escape from the boys that came along. After bringing in a load from the van, Sarah had told the boys she needed to check the place out for bathrooms, bedrooms and cooking materials. They'd agreed to finish it without her, and she'd almost skipped up the three stairs on the other side of the space that led to a door. Sarah proceeded to open the door directly in front of her, calling out her findings excitedly over her shoulder. "Bathroom. Huge tub, shower, toilet and vanity. Not too shabby."

I laughed as she closed the door and reached for the handle of the door to the left. "*Magic's balls!* Huge bedroom with two old style double beds, and two recliners facing the window. Perfect spot for a quiet chat with your roommate later if needed." Sarah stuck her head back out the door and winked. She really was a barrel of fun.

She stepped out of the bedroom and opened the door to the right of the bathroom. "Bedroom number two. Carbon copy of bedroom one." She closed the door and stood at the top of the stairs. "It looks like this place is perfectly set up for two couples. We should be so lucky."

I giggled, then almost choked as I noticed the two boys standing frozen in the doorway. "*Sar-ah*, exactly what couples would you be referring to, and who is the 'we' in *we should be so lucky?*" Sam asked, his eyebrows raised and a smirk on his face.

I seriously thought Sarah was going to fall flat on her face as she tripped down the few stairs and looked at Sam with a cheeky grin. "Oh, I assure you I wasn't referring to anyone here. I was just commenting on my observation of the available facilities. But as for the 'we', I'm pretty sure everyone here wouldn't mind having the perks that usually come with being part of a couple."

Everyone sat in stunned silence for a few seconds following Sarah's perky explanation. Exactly which part of her explanation each person chose to analyse was a mystery to me, and I would never admit where my thoughts had gone. But in the end, I think it was Sarah who started to laugh first at the absurdity of the entire situation, the rest of us not far behind her. Which was about when everyone seemed to decide to relax and take advantage of the short reprieve we all so desperately needed.

CHAPTER TWENTY-TWO

Tray

By the time we were all sitting around eating at the small dining table we'd found tucked away, everyone seemed to have finally relaxed, and we were all getting along like old friends. Sitting around drinking coffee while we all bantered had been fun, although it had become quite obvious that everyone avoided physical contact as much as we could.

It was like there was some kind of Mexican stand-off going on, where everyone was waiting for someone else to make the first move. Well, it sure wouldn't be me, cos I had no idea what was going on in my own head, let alone anyone else's.

"Okay," Sam said. "I guess I can be the one to address the elephant in the room. Tomorrow, we'll be heading into a situation we might not even make it out of. But the one thing that we will desperately need to know, is that we'll all have each other's backs. So, my vote is that we all go into this thing as a family."

"We've all been throwing around how we feel about our real siblings, and I believe we should try to start thinking about each other in the same way. That way, *if* we make it to this Immune sanctuary, not to mention if it even exists, we might all be in a better place to decide what we want our futures to look like. What do you think? Do you all think it's a workable scenario, or am I delusional even considering it might work?"

Strangely enough, Sam's idea seemed to remove a shitload of the pressure I'd been feeling. He was right. We all needed to be able to rely on each other one hundred per cent if we hoped to make it to Zion. And with the current *avoid-physical-contact-at-all-costs* situation, that was never going to happen.

"Yep, I'm in," I said, avoiding making eye contact with either of the girls. I'd be able to treat them the same as Emily and know that I wasn't being disloyal or not performing up to expectations towards anyone. And the funniest part was, that after all we'd been through, Sam and I weren't just going to be friends. We'd be brothers!

Sarah

MY BROTHER WAS A GENIUS! His plan wouldn't just put everyone's romantic issues on hold, I got the feeling that the situation we were walking into would solidify any doubts about who should be with whom. Something about embarking on trials that contained life and death situations usually had a way of bringing out one's true feelings.

What I found interesting, was that Tray seemed to deliberately avoid making eye contact with either Molly or me. As if we might judge him for being as emotionally screwed up as the rest of us. But the best part was, he was obviously questioning his feelings for Molly, which made me feel like I'd won the lottery. Playing happy families was a brilliant idea as far as I was concerned. 'Cos didn't brothers and sisters hug and tease each other and stuff? Definitely sounded right up my alley.

"Yep, I'm in too," I said and went back to eating my dinner. I tried not to laugh at the stunned silence as they waited for me to have more to say. "That is all," I couldn't help adding, just to put them out of their misery.

Molly

I DECIDED to follow Tray's lead and avoided making eye contact with anyone as I chewed on my lip. As far as I was concerned, Sam's plan was the perfect answer to all my problems. If they *both* started treating me just like their sister, it might make it easier in the long run to sort out exactly how I felt about each of them.

"Yep, I'm in three," I looked over at Sarah and smiled. "Besides, I already feel like Sarah and I were sisters in another lifetime."

When I finally decided to look around the table, I almost giggled at the relieved expressions on everyone's faces. Sam was right, it would be good to go into this unknown situation knowing we all had family at our backs. No more rivalry, or antagonism towards each other due to unresolved romantic entanglements.

Until now, I hadn't realised exactly how much grief the whole thing had been causing me, and it was nice to feel like a totally free agent who didn't have to worry about upsetting anyone as long as I had everyone's back equally.

Yep, I was ready to take on this challenge with my new family and find this place that had better exist or I'd be kicking a lot more arse, both magical and non-magical, before I was finished.

CHAPTER TWENTY-THREE

Sam

Well, that had all gone way better than I'd expected. In fact, the feeling of relief floating around the room was almost euphoric. Who knew that hitting the reset button on all our emotions was exactly what everyone in the room had wanted and needed?

I meant what I'd said about us all needing to go into this search with our heads screwed on the right way, but I had to admit that I was also counting on whatever trials we had to face helping us all to decide what we really wanted. But for now, I needed to do some very much overdue searches on The Glass House Mountains and their surroundings. From what I'd learned via a quick skim of the internet, the place was huge, with multiple entrances, and we had no idea where to even start.

"Okay, so now we have all that emotional stuff out of the way, I need to get a plan together for tomorrow so I can send out the broadcast to the rest of our former community." Using the word *former* to describe the people who, until today, I'd considered pretty much my only friends and family, made my gut clench painfully. It was just further proof that what I'd always known about this crappy world was true. *You could never* consider anyone or anything in your life permanent. Unless, of course, you were okay with losing it all in a heartbeat. Because that was our reality.

"Ooh, can I help?" Sarah's knee was jumping in her excitement, and I smiled at her unfeigned eagerness. "I have some maps already downloaded and I've found a few places with unusual names that might give us a hint about where we need to go."

I chuckled and pulled her chair over closer to mine. "No surprises there. So how about we put our heads together and see what we come up with. I'm always happy to share whatever clues that clever mind of yours has unravelled."

Molly cleared her throat. "Ummm, what if we all shared what we know and then see what different interpretations we all have to what we've found. Oh, only if you want to be involved as well, Tray. I didn't mean to assume..."

Tray held his hand up and smiled. "It's okay, Moll.

I'd love to be in on the brainstorming. Beats staring at the four walls."

I got up and went over to my backpack, rifling around until I found my notepad and pen. "Anyone else got a pen handy? It might be quicker if we all write down what we know first, then see what we end up with when we put it all together."

We all scrambled for our backpacks and miraculously each held up a pen. I tore four pieces of paper off the notepad and handed us each one. For the next ten minutes, we all sat and wrote down any thoughts we'd had about the upcoming journey, plus anything we'd found or heard about our destination. Then we lined up all four pieces of paper next to Sarah's phone, which was open to the map of the Glass House Mountains, and wracked our brains.

I was glad to see that every page held one thing the others didn't. Like Tray's suggestion that we each purchase and carry a knife at all times, something I probably wouldn't have considered until I'd wished I had one. I mean, I already had a gun, but knives were a lot quieter when needed.

"Okay, I'm so glad we did this," Sarah piped up. "Everyone has suggested something no one else thought of, so that's awesome. But it still all comes down to where we need to enter, or where to get information that might help. I have an idea, but it might be a longshot or just a coincidence."

"Oh, will you just spit it out Sarah," Molly said with

a grin. "You've been nearly jumping out of your skin since we started, so you must know it's something good."

Sarah laughed and poked her tongue out at me. "Smartie-pants," she said cheekily. "I was just trying to build up the tension. I mean, it's not like I was gonna get a drum roll or anything."

"*Sar-ah...*" I said, knowing how much she hated it when I drawled her name like that.

"Fine, fine," she said, pulling her paper and phone back in front of her. "I was originally thinking we should go in through the entrance at Beerwah, cos it's the biggest. But then, after zooming into the map a few times, I decided to check out the names of some of the smaller towns around the perimeter of the mountains themselves. Then I discovered that the entrance to one of the mountains, Mt Coonowrin, has been closed for years due to constant rockfalls and a few recorded deaths. Do you see where I'm going with this? Access denied and all that stuff?" She showed the notice on her phone around.

MOUNT COONOWRIN DECLARED A RESTRICTED AREA.

Unauthorised entry is strictly prohibited. For public safety, Magical Wards have been placed around the restricted access area shown on the map. Rocks and rock masses in this area are unstable and may fall without warning. Serious injuries and deaths have occurred here. Entry past this point or into any sections of the restricted access area is prohibited without a permit or written approval.

WHEN WE'D ALL SEEN it, she continued with her revelations. "Anyway, when I started looking around for somewhere we could stay that was near where this No Access sign was, I found a cute little farm stay called CIGAMON RETREAT. Ummm... notice anything unusual?"

Sarah had written the words in bold capitals, and we all gasped. No way... it couldn't be... could it?

"*Magic's balls, Sarah,*" Molly jumped up and ran around to hug Sarah. "That's NOMAGIC spelled backwards. You're a genius!"

And suddenly, we knew where we were going. I rang the Cigamon Retreat and asked if they had any accommodation available for the following two nights, making a booking for the four of us and checking whether there would be any other vacancies if our friends decided to join us. The woman laughed, and said they often catered to retreats, so had plenty of dormitory-style accommodation available. I thanked her calmly, then hung up and slapped the table with an exuberant "Yesssss".

"Oh, and I found this when I looked up Mount Coonowrin. Apparently, this guy climbed it before it was closed, so he posted this for any climbers who managed to get a pass to the restricted area. I'm thinking we head in the exact opposite direction to what he suggests. I mean this guy could be an Immune who posted this to direct people away from their vicinity."

Cross fence at end of Murphys Rd and follow track to base of mountain. Veer around left side of mountain towards southwestern corner.

"From there he just rabbits on about climbing the actual mountain, which I really don't think we'll have to do. After all, the only clue we have is that Zion is in the forest, which is around the *base* of the mountain. Well, that's what I'm hoping, anyway, cos I really don't want to have to climb a mountain that falls apart daily."

Sarah's words, along with the look of distaste on her face, made me laugh. But seriously, she was amazing to have found all this on her own. As always, I thanked whatever deity was listening that she'd been with me through all the crap said deity had thrown my way.

Okay, so Tray's dad said that the Immune Community was hidden somewhere in a forest at the Glass House Mountains. So, we'd found a retreat with an anagram of No Magic in its name, near the entrance to a closed mountain trail, which ran through a forest in the Glass House Mountains. This had to be it! Maybe this Zion place really did exist. Well, we'd know soon enough.

CHAPTER TWENTY-FOUR

Sarah

Okay, it was time to send the details of where to meet the following day to our friends from the former Immune Community. I shuddered at the word former and hoped we'd see them all soon. As always, the text would only contain a series of numbers, made up of the date, time and longitude and latitude coordinates. It was how we always communicated, just in case a phone fell into the wrong hands.

I'd seen quite a few skeptical looks on the faces of some of our Immune friends when Sam had told them about our proposed journey to find Zion, a refuge that may not even exist. Would I risk everything on a hope and a dream if not for the support of my new family? After all, the rumour about the place's existence could have been started by the Mage Council as a way to trap

Immunes. Oh Fates, what if that was true? We'd be responsible for leading them all to their death, or worse.

No, I couldn't let the doubts creep in now. Not when everyone had looked so excited when I'd moved to the lounge to send out the group text. I just had to believe that whatever deity was in charge of our fate out there in the universe had finally decided to give us a break. Holding my breath, I pressed send, and prayed we were doing the right thing.

Molly stood from the table and stretched her arms over her head. "Well, I think I've had enough excitement for one day. I'm off to bed, and I'll see you all in the morning." She threw me a surreptitious wink and headed to our room.

"Yep, me too," I said, covering my mouth and pretending to yawn.

"Oh, that's just great," Tray said, also standing from his chair and moving over to the lounge. He flopped onto the two-seater, pulling his legs up onto it and crossing them at his ankles. "So, my newly appointed brother and I get to bond, all on our own."

I tried to look sympathetic, but a giggle escaped anyway. "I'm sure you'll be fine. 'Night." I turned and hurried up the stairs, waving as I followed Molly into our room and pulled the door closed behind me.

"Night girls. Sleep well," Sam called, his words only just penetrating the closed door.

"Finally!" Molly said, moving to one of the recliners

and throwing herself down. "I was starting to think we'd never get out of there."

"Same," I said, flopping down next to Molly. "Although, I'm thinking tonight's heart-to-heart might have changed a bit since Sam's whole *let's-all-be-brothers-and-sisters* talk."

Molly chuckled. "Yeah, that was interesting, eh? Although, I have to admit, it's certainly taken the pressure off about who I'll upset next."

I decided it was time we both aired our feelings and saw what came out. Molly was apparently as desperate as I was to sort out our emotional baggage. "Okay, so let's say we talk about how we were feeling *before* the whole Happy Family thing?"

"To be honest, I think it might be more about what's going on in those two boys' brains. In a nutshell, I thought I was falling for Tray, until I met Sam. Now I think my feelings for Tray were, sort of, amplified by what we were going through and the fact that he was the only guy who'd ever been nice to me, not to mention the hottest guy I'd ever met. I mean, what if we kiss and there are no fireworks? What if we were just meant to be best friends? And then there's Sam..." Molly sighed, and her eyes took on a dreamy look.

"Oh boy, and I thought I had it bad. I have to ask, did you even notice that I'd started to develop feelings for Tray, no matter how hard I fought against it?"

Molly just stared at me and then burst out laughing. Yeah, she was right. The whole situation had become utterly ridiculous. And then I was laughing, too. We both laughed until the tears poured down our faces, each begging the other to stop so we could breathe. But every time one of us got the words out, the other just laughed harder. Yep, all the stress and fear of the last few days had finally pushed us both over the edge into insanity.

Tray

So, Sam had actually pushed the reset button on everything romance-related. How did I feel about that? Well, to be honest, it was kind of a relief. The stress from everything we were going through just to survive was enough to do a person's head in. Trying to sort through our emotional attachments to each other could definitely go on the backburner for a while, at least until we got to wherever we were going, or discovered it didn't exist.

I'd been trying not to let my mind go down that path, the one where we learned that our haven didn't exist. Because, well… what the hell would we do if that became our reality? It wasn't like we could just turn around and say *Oh well, that didn't work. Time for Plan B.*

Because there was no damned plan B, or any other letter of the alphabet. Everything was based on finding a positive outcome from Plan A.

To be honest, the only reason I hadn't lost the plot was that it had been Dad who'd told us about Zion. Of all the people in my world, I'd always had complete faith in my dad. Surely, he wouldn't have sent us on some wild goose chase if he'd doubted the information was real. Or had he just been grasping at straws because there were no other options?

"Hey… mind if I join you?"

Snapped out of my internal reverie, I watched Sam flop into the lounge opposite where I sat. As always, Sam looked as cool as a cucumber, with no sign of the stress I was currently wallowing in.

"So how do you do it, man?" I asked.

"Do what?" Sam asked, looking genuinely surprised.

"Stay calm and always manage to look completely in control."

Sam just laughed and sunk further back into the lounge. "Well, it's good to know that I come across that way. Guess I've had quite a few years to perfect the façade the world gets to see. Truth is, I'm terrified that I'll be leading all those people to their deaths tomorrow."

Sam's heartfelt words gave me a new grudging respect for this man. Sure, I was surprised he'd admitted his true feelings to *me*, the guy who'd done nothing but sneer at him since we met. But it was his ability to appear strong for all those around him that really sat me on my arse. Here I was, sitting and wallowing in self-pity about what would happen to *me* if this all went pear-shaped, while Sam was focused on keeping up a brave front and worrying about everyone else's well-being.

"Well, maybe it's time I took a page out of your book and pulled my head out of my own butt. I mean, seriously, sometimes I think I'll go insane with all the doubts and fears rolling around inside my head. Not to mention that, unlike you, the whole world can see how *I'm* feeling."

"You know. I'm starting to think we might have got off on the wrong foot. Maybe we'll work better together as brothers, rather than rivals," Sam said, keeping his eyes on his hands. "At least for now anyway."

I chuckled. "Yeah, yeah I know you're right. I guess it's time we just got on with it then."

Sam looked up and gave me the friendliest smile I'd ever received from him. And suddenly, nothing seemed as bad as it had before. Sam was right. If we all worked together, we might actually survive this nightmare.

CHAPTER TWENTY-FIVE

Sam

Before the sun had even risen the next day, we were all packed up, in the van, and on our way to the Glass House Mountains. Even though I'd enjoyed our short break and felt better about the emotional situation between us all, I was still relieved to be back on the road.

To say I'd been surprised by the conversation I'd had with Tray the previous evening would be an understatement. I mean, I kinda already knew that if our feelings for Molly weren't getting in the way, we'd probably have ended up good friends. Even though we were very different people who'd lived totally different lives until we met, our core values were pretty much identical. We were both prepared to do whatever it took to protect those we loved, and we both wanted payback for what the Magics had put us through. So, all in all, I was feeling a lot more positive about the future than I had twenty-four hours ago.

"So, it's only like an hour's drive to Beerwah. We won't be going through any cities or major towns, but is there anything from our lists we might need to grab in one of the smaller towns?" Sarah asked from the driver's seat. We'd all agreed that having a magic behind the wheel might help to disguise us if we needed it.

I had to smile when Molly started to rifle through her backpack for the lists we'd made up the previous night. She sat beside Sarah in the front passenger seat, and I was surprised she didn't have the lists stuck to the front windscreen. Then I really laughed, as I realised the only reason she didn't was probably because we had nothing to stick it on with.

Molly froze with her hand still inside the backpack and turned to me with a glare. "And what, exactly, do you find so amusing? Care to share with the rest of the class?"

Which just made me laugh even more. Okay, maybe it was the stress turning me into a blithering idiot, but I couldn't stop… for the life of me.

"Sam? What's going on? You're starting to worry me here, bro," Sarah said with a worried frown.

"Damn. Whatever it is, it must be good," Tray said, throwing me an evil wink from where he sat against the side of the van opposite me. "Cos Mr Joviality is not a nickname I'd *ever* consider for you!"

Finally getting myself back under control, I held my aching stomach with one hand and raised the other. "Okay… okay. Just stop, will ya? I may have just slightly overreacted to a thought I had. No biggie."

"You can't seriously believe we're gonna let you get away without sharing, do you?" Molly huffed indignantly. "Because I get the distinct impression that this thought had something to do with *me*. Am I right?"

"Seriously… can't a man have a personal thought every now and then without having to broadcast it to the whole damn world?"

"No!" Three voices said at once, and I knew I was beaten. I shrugged and told them what I'd been thinking. When I was finished, they all just stared at me. *What, were they waiting for the punchline or something?*"

"Well, I never said any of you would think it was funny. So, can we please just move on and forget about the entire episode?"

Molly was the first to react, and she started to giggle. "Sounds like I should add sticky tape to the list of essential items I need to carry at all times." Her words totally broke the tension in the air, and then we were all laughing.

When we'd all finally pulled ourselves back together, I remembered what had brought the whole thing on in the first place. "So, just to rewind a bit, I'm thinking we should wait until we get to Cigamon to look for all the stuff on the lists. After all, the town is at the base of the mountains, so it's sure to have at least one store that supplies everything the avid climber/trekker needs."

"Good," Sarah said when she was able. "I'd rather not have to stop at all before Cigamon. The fewer people we interact with along the way, the fewer clues we leave for the Councillors who are more than likely following us by now."

"Yep, I'm with you guys all the way," Tray said. "This van just changed from an all stations to an express. You hear that, Sarah? Cigamon… or bust."

Molly

THE SMALL TOWN of Cigamon was even smaller than I'd expected. As we drove down what appeared to be the main street, we passed a small supermarket that doubled as a post office, a café, a petrol station, and, of course, the sports store we'd been hoping for.

"Well, it looks like it's our lucky day," Sarah said as she slowed. "The café is actually open. Anyone else feel the need for coffee and some breakfast?"

"Just park the damn car, Sarah. You know we're all

hanging for sustenance just as much as you," Sam said, an impatient tone to his voice.

"Sheesh, you don't have to bite my head off, bro. We're on the same side, remember?" Sarah said as she pulled the van into a parking spot out the front of the café.

"Yeah, sorry, Sar, I didn't mean to snap. I just have a lot on my plate… ya know?" Sam said as he opened the sliding side door of the van.

By the time I stepped out of the van, Sarah was standing by the open sliding door. "It's okay, Sam. I was just pulling your chain. But just remember, we're all stressed and out of sorts, so we all need to be patient with each other."

Sam pulled her in for a hug, and I was shocked by the surge of jealousy his actions invoked. I mean, I knew my jealousy wasn't for the usual reasons. It was more that I'd have given just about anything to have someone hug me like that right then. Feeling stupid for my reaction, I tore my eyes away from the poignant scene and headed inside the café.

"Good morning," an elderly woman in an apron said as I entered the small shop. "Will your friends be joining you?" She nodded to the doorway.

"Yes, they're coming now. Do we just sit anywhere?" I asked. Looking around at the four tables taking up the entire space.

"Yep, wherever you like. You just passing through, or planning to stay in town for a while?"

Shit, what was I supposed to say again? Something about a planned meet-up with old friends?

"We're booked into the Cigamon Retreat for a couple of nights," Sam said as he crossed the room. "Meeting up with some old friends we haven't seen in a while."

I sagged in relief, falling into the closest chair and throwing Sam a grateful smile.

"Good morning," Tray said, pulling out the chair next to me. "Is there a menu, or do you just tell us what you have? 'Cos I could eat an elephant about now."

"Well," the woman replied. "How about full breakfasts all around? All the usual favourites piled high on a large plate."

Sarah groaned and gave the woman a huge smile. "That sounds absolutely amazing. What about coffee? Can we get that, too, please?"

The older woman just chuckled and patted Sarah's shoulder. "Of course. I have a fresh pot brewed out back. Now, you just sit down, and I'll get this all organised. Are there any special requests for the eggs? Sunny side up is the regular."

A chorus of, *yes, please, that's fine* and *perfect* came from around the table. The woman just nodded, turned and went out a door at the back of the café.

"I hope she's an example of the rest of the people here in Cigamon. I don't think I've ever felt so pampered," I said quietly.

"You're not alone there," Tray said. "Nothings aren't exactly treated with respect anywhere I've ever been."

"Well, considering the name of the town, one might assume this place has more than a few residents like us."

The door to the back room edged open, and Tray jumped up to help as soon as he saw the woman. She was balancing a tray carrying cups, milk and sugar on one hand, and holding the coffee pot with the other.

"Oh, thank you, son," the woman said as Tray relieved her of the tray. "It's nice to see that manners haven't become *completely* obsolete."

Tray placed a cup in front of each of us and the milk and sugar on the table. Within seconds, our cups were full, and we were all sighing with pleasure at the caffeinated goodness.

"You drink up now," the woman said. "Breakfast won't be long." Then she placed the half-empty coffee pot on the table and went back out to the kitchen.

"Magical balls," Sarah moaned. "Has coffee always tasted this good, or is this just the best coffee ever made?"

"Yeah, I think maybe a bit of both, Sar," I said, sharing in her blissful state.

"Bloody hell, you two," Sam said with a smirk. "It's just coffee, ya know."

"Ahhh, but coffee this good is a rare treat. And who knows how long it will be before we get anything even half as good. Does *trekking through the mountains for who knows how long* ring any bells?" Sarah's grin was almost evil.

"Fine. You've made your point. I shall relish the taste of all things sustenance-related while the opportunity exists," Sam said with a regal tone before giving his sister a flourishing bow. Well, as flourishing as you could get while sitting cramped at a table.

The smell of cooking eggs, bacon, sausages and whatever other ingredients constituted the café's full breakfast wafted from the kitchen. Tray was up on his feet again the minute the door began to open, and I wondered how much of his chivalry had to do with helping the woman and how much was a ploy to get his food quicker.

Either way, it wasn't long before there was a relaxed silence around the table as we all devoured the massive meals that had been placed in front of us.

CHAPTER TWENTY-SIX

Sarah

By the time we all piled back into the van, everyone was complaining that their tummies hurt. In all fairness, it had been the biggest meal I'd ever been served, and I'd enjoyed every mouthful. So, yep, I was paying the price too.

As we headed out of town in the direction the woman from the café had told us led to the retreat, I couldn't help thinking how different everything had been since Sam's ban on romantic feelings had come into being. Gone was all the tension and angst that had surrounded us all since we'd met.

Sure, I might have been guilty of checking out Tray's hot body when nobody was looking. Or silently pining for a little flirtatious play. But overall, everyone seemed to have successfully pushed all those feelings away into a box to be dealt with another day. *And wouldn't* that *day be a whole lot like Christmas!*

Well, at least the retreat wasn't hard to find. I turned off and drove through the wooden archway under a huge sign that read *Welcome to Cigamon Retreat.*

"Wow, somebody sure wants people to know they're here," Tray said, meeting my eyes in the rear-view mirror as he leaned up between the front seats to get a better view.

"Ya think?" I replied, smiling into those gorgeous blue eyes.

As we neared the front door, a middle-aged couple emerged from inside and gave us a wave.

"Hey, Moll, I guess that answers your question about everyone here being friendly. I don't know of many places where the hosts greet their guests at the front door," I said, throwing Molly a smile.

Molly chuckled. "Yeah, I really want to say that things just keep getting better and better, but I don't want to jinx us."

"Ummm… sorry to be the bearer of bad tidings, Molly, but I'm pretty sure you just said it," Sam said, reaching over to pat her shoulder from where he'd now joined Tray.

"Damnit… I did, too. So do you think keeping my fingers crossed might negate the jinx?" She blushed and then laughed, and we all joined in.

The couple in the doorway were literally beaming by the time I pulled the van into a designated parking spot. "Okay, shorthand reminder of the plan. Find out everything, tell them nothing, got it?"

They all just shook their heads as they mumbled their agreement while clambering from the vehicle. I couldn't hold back the giggle when I heard Sam's *"Yes, Mum"* reply as he winked at me before sliding the door to the van open. And the reason I couldn't hold back the giggle? Because Sam knew it was exactly the kind of thing Mum would have said in the same situation.

"Good morning, and welcome to Cigamon Retreat," the woman cooed as we approached the verandah where they stood. "You must be the Kelly booking, I assume?"

Sam strode forward and held out his hand. "Good morning. Yes, I'm Sam Kelly, and this is my sister Sarah and our friends M… Mary and Tony."

Thank magic for Sam's quick thinking. We couldn't do much about the fact that Molly and Tray's descriptions were all over the media, but using their real names was definitely something we could avoid.

The man stepped forward and shook Sam's hand. "I'm Harry, and this is my wife, Paula. Pleased to meet you. Well, now that we've got all the niceties out of the way, how about you follow me, and we'll get all the paperwork out of the way? Then you can focus on the important stuff, like settling into your rooms."

"Thanks, that sounds great," Sam said with a smile as he followed Harry inside.

I hesitated, looking at Tray and Molly as if to ask them if we should follow Sam or just wait here.

Before we could decide, Paula piped up in her cheery voice. "Would you like to sit out here and wait for your friend? No point in you all crowding in there. There's a nice comfy outdoor lounge setting on the other side of the verandah."

"Awesome. Please, lead the way, and we'll follow," I said, relieved to have the decision made.

The instant we reached the end of the front verandah, I sucked in a breath. The view of the Mountains and the surrounding forests was absolutely spectacular. I stumbled over to the lounge setting and flopped down into a chair, noticing that Molly and Tray looked equally stunned.

Tray was the first to recover his voice. "That is, without a doubt, the most incredible view I have ever seen. It's truly magnificent."

"Well, I've lived here my entire life, so I can't say I've ever seen anything more beautiful either." Paula sat down on a chair opposite and smiled.

"Wait… you've never been out of Cigamon? Like *ever*?" Tray blustered.

"I've never had the desire to be anywhere else. I hear plenty of stories from friends who've travelled, and nothing I've ever heard has made me feel like I'm missing out on anything. Cigamon is where I was born, and it's where I intend to die. Like you said, what could be better than seeing that every day?"

Paula swept her arm across the panoramic view in front of us, and I had to agree with her. If I could choose where my future led, I had to admit that staying here, with Tray, Molly and Sam, would be pretty high up on my list of choices.

Tray

SITTING THERE on that verandah surrounded by friends while taking in the spectacular view in front of us, I had to agree with Paula. This place was about as close to paradise as you could get. But how long would it be before it was all ruined by the Magics descending on the town looking for us?

"I really envy you, Paula," Molly said with a heavy sigh. "I would give anything to be able to live out the rest of my life somewhere like this."

"So, what's stopping you then, sweetheart?" Paula asked, the sympathetic look in her eyes tinged with curiosity.

"I think what Mary means is that there's nowhere like this in the city where we live with our families," Tray jumped in at the slightly panicked look on Molly's face. "You're lucky you were born somewhere like this where your family is too."

Paula's face fell, and I wanted to kick myself for ruining her happy demeanour. "Unfortunately, Harry's the only family I have left now. My parents and siblings, well, let's just say they wanted to see the world. And Harry and I were never lucky enough to have children."

"Oh Paula, I'm so sorry," Molly said, her eyes glassy with unshed tears. "Are they… I mean, do you know…?"

"I never heard from them again. I've no idea where they are or if they're… well, let's just stick with not knowing where they are."

My heart went out to this poor woman. I knew exactly what it was like to lose family. And even as I railed against how unfair life had been to me, I knew my family were safer without me in their lives. Maybe one day…

A door opened behind where we sat, and Harry stepped out onto the verandah, followed by Sam. The absolutely dumbfounded look on Sam's face when he took in the view made me smile. Yep, even Sam was bowled over by the sheer magnificence before him.

"Wow…" was all he managed to say as he joined us. "I mean seriously… just wow."

Everyone laughed at Sam's profound words, or the lack thereof, and Harry moved over to place his hands on Paula's shoulders. "Well, you're all good to go. I've given Sam the keys, and instructions on how to get to your cabin. If you need anything, please feel free to ask."

We all scrambled to our feet without another word, obviously eager to get to our cabin and discuss what we'd learned.

Sam held up his hand, and we all stopped moving. "So… the cabin's not far. I think I might walk, and you guys can follow me in the van. I could do with some fresh air."

We'd reached the van, and I was about to open the sliding door when Molly grabbed my hand. "You know what? Why don't you hop in the front seat with Sarah? I'm going to walk with Sam. He really shouldn't be allowed to have all that fresh air to himself."

Before I could even open my mouth, Molly had called out to Sam to wait and hurried over to join him.

Sam

Okay, so I know it had been my idea to put all the romantic feelings away for now, but apparently my heart didn't get the memo. Because the sight of a rather flushed Molly hurrying towards me had my heart pounding in my chest. *Okay, dumbarse, cool your engines. Sister...remember?*

"Hey, I hope you don't mind," Molly said with a sheepish smile. "I couldn't stand the thought of climbing back into that van again either. So, you'll just have to share some of that fresh air you were talking about. Right, lead on, boss..."

"Hey, what's with the *boss* crap? No way I want to be considered in charge of this shitshow," I said, nudging her with my shoulder.

"Well, too bad, hotshot. You can't just step up when

you feel like it and not when you don't. Besides, I vote for you, and I'm sure the other two would agree."

Her grin was so cheeky that I couldn't resist returning it. "Is that right? So, does that mean you have to do everything I tell you to from now on? Hmmm?"

Damn, she was even more gorgeous when she blushed. But she wasn't going to back down that easily. "Only if your orders are in *everyone's* best interests."

Bloody cheeky minx had me there. No orders that might trifle with the current rules. In other words, nothing that might upset Tray.

"So," Molly said, linking her arm with mine like any brother and sister would do. "Did you learn anything from Harry?" *Oh, she was good.* She'd managed to steer the conversation away from the previous topic without even blinking.

"Well, he kind of hinted that all the residents here were Nothings, except for the few Magics who were like Sarah. I did tell him we wanted to do some hiking while we were here, and he said the sports store would have everything we needed. Then I asked how hard it would be to get a pass to visit Mt Coonowrin, and his eyes nearly popped out of his head. He just mumbled something under his breath and said he'd get back to me."

"That's great, Sam. His reaction sounds like exactly how an Immune would respond to hearing someone wanted to approach Zion. Do you think we should wait for him to come to us, or should we just throw caution to the wind and mention the Immune thing?" Molly was practically skipping with excitement, and I so didn't want to burst her happiness bubble. But we were a long way from risking telling anyone anything just yet.

"How about we wait until Tray and Sarah are around before we make any decisions? In fact, maybe it would be better if you just let me tell them and pretended you didn't already know. I'd rather not step on any toes if we can help it."

Molly stopped skipping, but her smile stayed in place. "See, that's why you're the perfect boss. You have this knack of knowing what to say and what not to say, depending on the situation."

Yep, I suppose Molly was right. Well, except where she was concerned, that is. Somehow every shred of diplomacy and reason flew out the window when the situation concerned Molly. *But I was working on controlling it... wasn't I?*

Sarah

THE LOOK on Tray's face as Molly ran off after Sam had been priceless. His head had swivelled from where I sat in the front seat to Molly's retreating form at least three times before he'd shrugged and opened the front passenger door.

"Guess it's just you and me then, Sar," Tray said as he settled into his seat. But when he lifted those penetrating blue eyes to look into mine, I wanted nothing more than to reach over and hug him. He looked so much like a lost puppy it was heartbreaking.

"Cool," I said, putting on my chipper voice. "Then let's get this show on the road."

Tray chuckled. "How is it that you can maintain such a positive outlook no matter what?"

I bit my lip and looked away, starting the van and crawling along behind Sam and Molly. "Did you ever consider that I might be faking it sometimes?" I replied before I could stop myself.

"Seriously?" Tray asked, looking totally surprised by my revelation. "Why would you do that?"

I just shrugged, wishing I could take the words back. I'd never told anyone that before, not even Sam. "I don't know, really. It's just something I've always done. I have a huge problem with any form of confrontation, as well as expressing who I really am. So, always appearing to be the happy one means I don't have to deal with those things very often. My mum used to tell me I was a *people-pleaser*."

Tray reached out and put his hand over mine on the steering wheel. "Well, if you ever need someone to let it all out to, I'm your man," Tray said softly. "I may not have magic, but I'm a good listener."

"Wait, why would it matter whether you had magic?" Surely Tray didn't feel that me having magic and him not having it made him inferior in some way. Well, it was time to correct *that* misconstrued belief. "To be honest, after spending so much time in the Immune community, I actually prefer those who *don't* have magic."

When he didn't say anything, I looked over to see Tray staring at me like I'd grown a second head. Then he broke into a huge smile. "Seriously? I mean, I just thought... well, it doesn't matter now, anyway."

Hell no! There was no way I was letting him get away with that feeble attempt at a reply. Was he saying that he didn't think *I* would be interested in *him* just because he didn't have magic? Every nerve ending in my body was tingling with anticipation. Did that mean he'd actually entertained the thought of developing feelings for me? *Holy snapping magic balls!*

Pushing my foot down gently on the brake pedal, I turned in my seat and looked directly into Tray's eyes. "I happen to have been very attracted to more than a few Nothings and Immunes over the years. *What* they are doesn't matter to me. I'm way more impressed by *who* they are. Unfortunately, the guy I *might* be interested in is hung up on someone else at the moment. But who knows... things can always change."

Before I could say anything else that might incriminate me, I turned back to the road and lifted my foot off the brake. Molly and Sam obviously hadn't even noticed we'd stopped.

Well, the ball was entirely in Tray's court now. I'd cleared up any and all misconceptions he might have had about how *I* felt, and now I was content to sit back and wait for whatever happened next. Whether he'd choose to pick up the ball and run with it was anyone's guess.

CHAPTER TWENTY-EIGHT

Molly

By the time we'd finished unpacking the van and sorting out who had what room, I was ready to do nothing for the rest of the day. Unfortunately, we still had the meet-up at Beerwah pub later that afternoon. And, of course, Sam was a stressed mess over the whole thing.

I sipped on my coffee as I sat on the lounge, taking in our new surroundings. We each had our own rooms —small but serviceable—and they all ran off this one central room. There were eight bedrooms altogether, so we'd taken the four all on the same side. The other four were available to whoever turned up at the meetup and needed them.

The room we were currently sitting in was huge, with a lounge suite and an open fire at each end of the room. In the centre of the room sat an enormous dining table with enough chairs to seat up to twenty people. Everything would have been great except for the two huge elephants in the room.

From the way Sam had been pacing around the room for the last hour, he felt personally responsible for the outcomes of both. Although I wasn't sure how it could be his fault alone if the Magics found them, or the other Immunes didn't come to the meet-up.

"Sam… for magic's sake bro, can you please sit down?" Sarah said in a calm, reasonable voice. "I'm getting dizzy from watching you go around and around this room. You know that stressing won't make anything better. Whatever is meant to happen, will. Regardless of the number of holes you wear into this carpet."

"Fine," Sam said, dropping onto one of the vacant seats. "But I can't just sit here and do nothing. How long until we have to be at the pub?"

"Another two hours, and Beerwah is only another twenty-minute or so drive," Sarah said. "Although, maybe it would be a good idea if we got there early and scoped out the place. Just in case our message leaked and there are any surprises waiting for us."

"Yep. I agree with Sarah," Tray said, sending a smile her way. "Better than sitting around here going crazy."

Sarah looked over to Sam and then to me. "Yeah, I'm fine with whatever," I said, happy to do anything to reduce some of the stress in the air.

"Fine," Sam huffed again, standing up and heading out the door towards the van.

"Talk about a limited vocabulary," Tray whispered as I was passing him. I punched him in the arm and gave him a filthy look. The last thing we needed was a problem between Sam and Tray. "Just get in the van, smartarse," I said, and walked out the door.

Tray

I couldn't get out of the van fast enough when we parked in a back street a block away from the Beerwah Pub. The tension in the van had been almost suffocating, and no one had even spoken the entire way. Pulling on the baseball cap I'd borrowed from Sam, I watched Molly tuck her hair up inside a beanie cap. I'd been meaning to suggest we change our hair colour or something to disguise our well-circulated descriptions, but this would have to do for now.

It was a relief to find that Beerwah was a much bigger town than Cigamon. Maybe we wouldn't stick out as badly as we had there.

"Now, just remember to keep a low profile," Sam said as Sarah locked the van. "We'll go straight to the dining room and do some snooping under the guise of studying the menu."

Everyone just nodded, and we all headed towards the entrance to the pub. Molly looked so pale and sickly that I linked my arm with hers and jiggled. "Hey, now who's being the complete worrywart? It's going to be fine. We're just some tourists stopping at the pub for dinner. Now just take a couple of deep breaths and try not to look quite so grim."

Molly broke into a smile, and I wanted to punch the air. No matter what was going on between us all, I could still cheer her up. "Thanks, Tray. You really are a good friend," Molly said, jiggling me back.

I was surprised to realise that Molly addressing me as her friend didn't hurt like it used to. Maybe we really were destined to just be good friends after all. And ever since the enlightening conversation I'd had with Sarah earlier, I was starting to believe that would be the best outcome all around.

The funniest part was that the two people walking in front of us would probably be very relieved to know I'd finally reached that conclusion.

Sam

IT DIDN'T TAKE LONG to work out that the pub was overflowing with Magics. My stomach churned with nausea at the thought of our friends walking into a situation like this. Hell, even the thought of *us* being there among so many magics was making me want to get up and run back to the van. It felt a bit like what I'd always imagined being stuck between a rock and a hard place would feel like. Damned if we do, and damned if we don't.

I almost fell out of my chair when Molly's hand slipped onto my leg. I looked up into her beautiful burnt-toffee coloured eyes and saw the worry there. Then she leaned over and whispered against my ear.

"I'm ready to do whatever you think will be best in the long run. There's still time to message everyone and abort the meeting."

I looked over at Tray and Sarah and knew they felt the same. So how the hell was I supposed to decide what to do? Why was it always me who had to make all the decisions? The burden of being the buck where everything stopped was really starting to piss me off.

Molly leaned away from my ear and looked me in the eye. Whatever she saw there seemed to make up her mind.

"Would anyone mind if I called it a night? I'm so sorry, but I'm suddenly feeling really nauseous," Molly said, reaching for her purse and standing up.

"Wait... we all came together," Sarah said. "How will you get back to the motel?"

"It's not that far. I can just walk. I'll probably be fine once I get back out in the fresh air."

Tray stood up and put down his menu. "No way you're walking home alone. I vote we all go, and we can get some take-away on the way home."

I sat in stunned silence as I watched the performance being put on by the other three people at the table. Damn, they were good. If I didn't know it was all a show, even I'd have believed it was all for real.

"Come on, Sam. I know you were looking forward to a steak, but we can always come back tomorrow night. When M… Mary is feeling better."

Before I could even speak, Molly was pulling me from my chair, and we were following Tray and Sarah out of the pub. Still unsure if we'd escaped unnoticed, no one spoke until we were in the van and on our way back to Cigamon.

"Molly… you are a genius!" Sarah squealed as she drove back to Cigamon.

"You can talk!" Molly practically squealed back. "It was like you'd been handed a script and someone called 'action'. And as for Tray and his promise to go back tomorrow night? Absolutely priceless."

So what had I done to help? Absolutely nothing but sit there like a stunned mullet and watch. "I'm sorry, guys," I said quietly.

"Don't you dare apologise, Sam. I only did what I did because I knew we all agreed it was the best way to handle the situation. If you'd had to make the decision, and anything went wrong, you'd have taken all the blame upon yourself. We're a team, a family, and there will be no *I told you so* or *this is all your fault* on my watch."

Silence hung in the air for a minute, and then everyone burst out laughing. Watching Molly in protective mode was an incredible sight, and if it were possible, I fell even harder for the girl I might never have.

CHAPTER TWENTY-NINE

Sarah

My first thought when I woke the following morning was the memory of Molly at the pub. We'd all been able to see how much Sam was struggling with the decision to go or stay, and Molly had just stepped up and owned it. I also knew that Sam had appreciated what we'd done.

The sound of someone pounding on the front door had me wide awake and jumping out of bed. No one else seemed to be around, so I pulled on a robe and hurried to open the door at the far end of the room. Paula stood in the doorway, wringing her hands.

"Ummm, sorry to bother you so early, but Harry asked if you could all come up to the main house as soon as possible."

Just like that, Sam was standing beside me, pulling

his t-shirt over his head. "Why? What's going on?" he asked, rubbing at his bed-hair.

"I…I… please, just come. We'll explain everything when you get there. I'll see you soon." Paula turned and hurried off towards the main house.

"What the hell was that all about?" Tray said as he walked towards us. He too was pulling on his T-shirt and *hubba-hubba*, I was trying not to salivate at the sight of his slowly disappearing abs.

Finally, Molly emerged from her room, already dressed and ready for the day. I looked down at my singlet and sleep shorts with the almost threadbare robe over the top and felt like a total loser. Until I caught Tray checking me out in my skimpy sleep attire and my care factor plummeted to zero immediately.

"What did I miss?" Molly asked, taking in the bedraggled state of the three of us. "I just got back from a nice long morning walk."

"Harry wants to see us all up at the main house as soon as possible," I said, backing into my room to get dressed. "No idea why, but Paula was a mess. I'll be back in a minute."

I closed the door and rifled through my backpack for some clean clothes. I'd planned to do some laundry this morning, but who knew if that would be possible after this? *What in the name of magic balls was going on now?*

After quickly running a hairbrush through my hair, I opened my door to find everyone else dressed and ready to go. The worried frowns on all their faces probably matched mine.

"Okay, let's go," Sam said, and we followed him out the door and along the road to the main house. I could have kissed Paula when I smelled the aroma of freshly brewed coffee coming from where she stood on the verandah. But one look at Harry's face where he stood beside her had my stomach in knots. Something was very wrong, and we were about to find out what.

"Please," Paula said with a slight waver in her voice. "Everyone, just grab a coffee and sit. We don't have a lot of time."

We all looked at each other and decided not to ask what she meant. It was pretty obvious we'd know what was going on soon enough.

"Right," Harry said, and I noticed he'd chosen not to sit. "I'm sorry we disturbed you so early, but as Paula said, we don't have much time." Sam looked about to ask what he meant by that, but Harry raised a hand. "Okay, let's start by all throwing our cards on the table. First of all, Paula and I are both Immunes, and I'm assuming you all are, too."

Everyone looked to Sam and he nodded. Harry let out a heavy sigh.

"And *Mary* and *Tony* are the two runaways the Magic Council have been searching for?"

Again, Sam nodded but didn't speak. "Then the situation is exactly as I thought. We've received word that Beerwah is currently being searched from top to bottom. Apparently, they heard you were holed up in a motel there somewhere." If the situation hadn't been so dire, I'd have high-fived Molly for mentioning the motel.

"I gather you were in town last night?"

"Yeah, we—" Harry brushed away Sam's words.

"I'm sorry, son, but none of that matters now. It won't take those Magics long to discover you're not in Beerwah, and we're the next stop." Harry reached behind him and grabbed a large backpack with tools of every description hanging off it. "I had four of these made up for you last night, and I'm glad I did. Because you need to leave… *now*."

"But what about our stuff back at the cabin?" Molly asked, staring at the pack Harry held.

"Paula and I will erase all signs that you were ever here, including hiding the van somewhere." He reached into his pocket and pulled out a folded paper. "This is the best I can do with directions. We've never been there, but none we've given this map have ever returned. Which means they either found Zion, or… well, let's not dwell on any other possibilities."

Sam reached out and took the map from Harry, then shook the man's hand. "Thanks for all your help. I don't know how we can ever repay you."

"Oh psshhtt, that'll be enough of that. You kids need to get going, and we'll make sure there are no tracks to follow," Paula said with a small smile. "Good luck, and I hope to see you all again someday."

Molly threw her arms around Paula and thanked her, and then I did the same. Tray shook Harry's hand, and it was time for us to go. Although, now it was time to actually begin the journey we'd been planning, I suddenly felt like I wasn't ready. I'd sent a message to our Immune friends the previous night saying to stay where they were and keep safe until they heard from us again. And now I wanted nothing more than to be with them wherever they were.

Feeling eyes on me, I looked over to where Tray stood, pulling his backpack on, and our eyes met. *You okay?* he mouthed with a soft smile.

I returned his smile and nodded, feeling better knowing that Tray was watching out for me. I shrugged the heavy backpack on and looked over at Sam. He was studying the map, the intense look on his face making me nervous all over again. What was he seeing that made him look that tense?

"Okay, everybody ready to go?" Sam asked, pushing the map into his jeans pocket and shrugging on his own backpack.

Ready as I'd ever be...

Molly

WE'D BEEN WALKING for a couple of hours when I decided that Harry must have stuffed my backpack with rocks. The damn thing weighed a ton, and my shoulders were starting to ache already. What in the world had made us think we could even attempt what we were about to do? None of us had any experience with hiking or climbing or even *surviving* in this kind of terrain. Or any other, for that matter.

"How you holding up?" Sam asked, pushing back a branch as I ducked to get past him.

"Yeah, I think it might be best for everyone if I don't answer that question," I replied with a grimace.

"That bad, huh?" he chuckled.

"Let's just say I've never really been a fan of the great outdoors. Which makes *this* place complete and utter overkill."

"Okay, so maybe if we talked about something else, it might take your mind off it?" Sam suggested.

"Did you have a particular topic in mind?" I asked with a raised eyebrow.

"Well, as a matter of fact—" I assumed Sam's words were cut off by the same feeling that had just washed over me. There was magic being used somewhere nearby, and it felt like way more than any one person could wield.

"Did you feel that?" Tray asked, hurrying to catch up to us.

"Feel what? The magic in the air? Since when can

you three feel magic that's not being used on you?" Sarah said from behind Tray.

Ho-ly shit! Sarah was right. How *could* we feel this magic in the air? I sucked in a deep breath and realised that this magic smelled different. I'd never smelled anything like it. And it seemed to just be hanging in the air all around us.

"I know this sounds weird, but this magic feels different to anything I've ever felt before, Sam said, scratching his head. "Like, maybe it's not coming from a person?"

Sarah looked around at all of us and shrugged. "Well, there's one sure way to find out what's going on. I don't know about the rest of you, but I'm just gonna follow my nose."

Then she was diving into the bush to the right of where we'd been walking without another word.

"Hey, wait up," Tray called as he followed after Sarah's rapidly disappearing back. "Come on, you pair, I don't really think it would be a good idea to get separated right now."

"I think he may be right," Sam grinned and bowed, sweeping an arm across in front of him. "After you, my lady."

Of course, I was blushing profusely as I followed after Tray, listening to Sam's chuckle as he followed me. *Stop blushing, you idiot. No romantic notions, remember?* I wanted to smack myself in the forehead, but didn't want to give Sam any more reasons to chuckle at my expense.

Less than five minutes later, I almost walked into Tray's back. "Hey, a bit of notice that you're stopping next time, please?" Sam's hand fell on my shoulder as he nodded to where Tray and Sarah both stood frozen, staring into the clearing ahead of them.

"What in all the magical dungheaps is that?" Sarah whispered, the awe in her voice evident.

My eyes felt like they'd narrowed to pinpoints as I took in the unexplained presence before us. It was like an oversized door made of nothing but light and magic. Whatever the hell it was, I was struggling to resist the urgent pull it exuded. Everything else around me faded into insignificance as I moved toward the magic that beckoned me, and I welcomed the thin strands of what could only be magic that reached out and wrapped around me.

I was vaguely aware that someone was trying to pull me back, but they seemed to just fall away when the magic touched me. The voices, too, calling out to me seemed to get further and further away the closer I got to the door. Then, before I'd had a conscious thought about what was happening, I was sucked into the doorway and everything went dark.

CHAPTER THIRTY

Tray

"Molly, noooo…" I knew there was no point yelling. No way Molly could hear me. My voice was hoarse from all the yelling I'd been doing since Molly pushed past me and started heading toward the… whatever it was.

The next thing I knew, Sarah's arms were wrapped around me as the tears began to fall. "Hey, it's okay. She'll be okay. We just have to believe that."

I looked over to Sam, who sat sprawled on the ground with his head hung low. "I couldn't stop her. The damned magic actually worked on me. How is that even possible?"

"Well, you did say it felt different to any magic you'd ever felt before. But it didn't seem to want to hurt Molly. It just wanted her to go with it," Sarah said, laying her head against my chest, as if she, too, needed the contact.

"So what the hell are we supposed to do now?" Sam asked, brushing himself off as he stood. "Something tells me the magic won't let anyone else enter."

Sarah shrugged, and then as if she'd just realised where she was, she pulled away from me. I missed the contact immediately, and didn't even feel guilty for wanting to pull her back into my arms.

"We wait," Sarah said. She looked around where we stood and pointed to the far side of the clearing. "I vote we set up camp and at least make ourselves comfortable. Who knows how long we'll have to wait."

Sam's eyes were still glued to the spot where Molly had disappeared. He looked like he was trying to will her to come back out. Which was when it finally hit me that the situation had changed for all of us. Sam hadn't just been flirting with Molly to get up my nose. He was head over heels crazy about her, and instead of the jealousy I'd expected to feel at that thought, I only felt sympathy for my new friend. And yes, somewhere along the line we had become friends.

With a huge sigh of resignation, Sam picked up his and Molly's backpacks and trudged over to where Sarah had suggested we set up camp. It was pretty close to lunchtime anyway, so we all agreed to use the time to eat and drink. As I sat down on a log and started to rifle through my backpack, I realised for the first time that we hadn't even checked to see what was inside them. We'd all been too busy trying to put as much space as possible between us and the retreat.

"Wow, whoever packed these bags did a brilliant job. I can't think of anything that was on our list that isn't in here. And we didn't even have to shop... *score*," Sarah said, her voice muffled as her head almost disappeared inside the backpack.

"Damnit, Sarah," Sam said with a growl. "How can you be so chipper after what just happened? Don't you even care that Molly could be... well, something not good."

Sarah stood and put her hands on her hips. "Okay, brother of mine. You need to listen and listen good. What do you think just happened over there? Have you considered the fact that we already know Molly has a unique relationship with magic? She has a power no one has ever seen before. And the magic didn't seem to be even the slightest bit interested in any of us. So... maybe the magic has something it needs Molly to know. I just have this feeling in my gut that she'll come back out as soon as she's learned what she needs to know. Okay?"

I tried really hard to hide my smile at the look on Sam's face when Sarah finished her tirade. "Seriously?" Sam fumed. "You just 'figured it all out' without actually knowing anything? What if you're wrong?"

"Then I will be just as pissed and sad as you two. But I refuse to go down that road until we *know* my theory is wrong. Now can you please just shut up and let the rest of us eat our lunch."

There was no point denying it any longer—Sarah was magnificent. And the feelings I had for her and Molly were as different as chalk and cheese. There was no doubt in my mind that I loved them both, but in very different ways. Sure, Molly was beautiful and smart and funny, but there was no passion or desire in my feelings for her. Okay, so maybe I'd thought about kissing her when we first met, but now it felt like I'd be kissing my sister.

Then there was Sarah, also beautiful, smart and funny. But Sarah was just something…more. I suddenly realised I'd been pushing the feelings away because I'd been so sure she wouldn't be interested in me. Not to mention the confusion over my feelings for Molly.

Which had me wondering how many people 'settled' for the one they weren't meant for. Maybe I was just one of the lucky ones who'd met their soulmate before they were committed to someone else. I mean, not that I'd have been unhappy with Molly. But that was only because I hadn't found the real thing to compare it to.

Damn, who was this person invading my brain? I sounded like some kind of philosophical nerd trying to solve the mysteries of the universe. Who cared how, or why, or what if? Sarah had all but told me how she felt, so what was stopping me from moving forward? *Molly.* I needed to talk to her and explain what I was feeling. I was pretty sure she was stuck in the exact same situation I'd been in. And it was time to clear the air.

If she ever came back...

CHAPTER THIRTY-ONE

Molly

$\mathcal{I}$ tried to open my eyes so I could figure out where I was. But the light surrounding me was so bright it almost blinded me.

She wakes, I heard a hissing voice that sounded like it was inside my head.

The light is too bright for her eyes, another voice practically wheezed.

Wait. How did they know the light was too bright? I hadn't said… ah shit. They really were inside my head.

Then subdue the lighting so she may see. I wasn't sure whether this was a different voice or the same one I'd heard first, but suddenly, I had no desire to open my eyes anymore. Maybe I could just keep them closed and see what happened if I tried to 'think' back at them.

They obviously didn't want me dead, or I would be already.

Who are you, and where am I? I thought, and a soft tittering began in my head. Were they discussing how to answer me?

You are here, and we are the Source.

Well, didn't *that* just explain everything… *not.*

Ummm… sorry, but I need a bit more information. Exactly where is here? And the Source of what?"

The answer to your question is not easily explained. In a sense, we are everywhere, and you are inside that everywhere. We are the Source of all magic.

My head felt ready to explode, and my curiosity was making it harder to keep my eyes closed every second. Okay, so they were saying I was literally *inside* magic. How was that even possible? And all that aside, I was Immune to magic. How had they even brought me here?

Aah, but that is where you are wrong, little Saviour. You are far from being just an Immune. You are unique. You are not a magic, nor are you a Nothing or an Immune. Let's just say for now, you are Something, with the potential to become Everything.

It was quickly becoming obvious that I'd ingested some form of hallucinogenic sometime in the last few hours. Because what these… *voices* were saying was absolutely insane. I'd never have guessed my mind was even capable of conjuring up this kind of loop-de-loop craziness. And what was with the 'little Saviour' thing?

I was about as far from being a saviour as a newborn puppy!

Hmmm... I see that your mind is refusing to accept our words as reality. Perhaps if we activated some of the memories in your psyche that have been blocked?

What the hell? No way... get out of my—the thought halted as an image appeared inside my head like I was replaying memories I didn't know I had.

Wait, it wasn't me watching. It was a young girl about my age but dressed in a fashion I'd never seen before. And *I* was inside *her* head. Then she heard the voices, which of course meant I did too.

"It is done," one voice said in a flat monotone. "The Guardians are all dead. Except those few assigned to duty who missed the feast."

"Excellent," a different, more shrill voice, excitement lacing his words. "She'll have no one to hide behind this time. Her reign is finally at an end. See that the remaining Guardians are dealt with and have them replaced by Magics who are loyal to the cause. This ends today."

I never saw either of the men whose voices I'd heard, but I was suddenly ripped from the memories to another place where a beautiful woman sat listening to the young girl, who was also me, telling her what she'd seen.

"Aah, so the words of the prophecy have come to pass. Do not look so sad, little one. We all knew this day would come. But unlike the Grand Vizier believes, it will not be the end. Another will come and restore order among the chaos. She will be magic's saviour, with powers beyond anything ever seen before." I flinched at the sound of pounding on the door across from where we stood. The young girl's face was streaked with tears as the men broke through the door, and the vision abruptly ended. To be honest, I was relieved. I didn't need to see what happened next.

Then it hit me why I'd seen this vision. *Hell. To. The. No!*

Wait, wait... you think I'm the one they were talking about? I'm not a saviour's bootlace. Besides, who or what am I even saving? What happened that day?

What you just saw was the day magic everywhere was enslaved by a group of corrupt Magics. What you now know as the Magical Council.

I sucked in a shocked breath, forgetting all about keeping my eyes closed. The light wasn't as bright as it had been before, but the whole idea I'd had of seeing where I was now proved ridiculous. It was like I was floating in some kind of suspended animation made completely of light. Yep, now I understood why they'd had so much trouble explaining where I was.

So, just hold on there one more minute. You think I'm going to overthrow the Magical Council?

The tittering I'd heard before now sounded a hell of a lot like giggles. Were they seriously laughing at me?

Not alone, little Saviour. In fact, the community of Zion you currently seek has been preparing for the day you arrive for many years. You can expect a warm welcome. We just felt you should know a little more about the past before you arrived.

What about my friends? How am I supposed to explain all this to them?

What you tell your friends is entirely up to you. But they too will play an important role in the coming battle.

Bloody hell. For the gazillionth time I wondered why my life always had to be so complicated.

Because you were born for glory, little one. And that road is never easy. Now, I believe it is time to return you to your friends.

Wait, before you do, I said, wanting to know just one more thing I hadn't figured out. *Who were all the people in that room, and how did they die?*

They were the Guardians of Magic, they were poisoned at a celebratory feast, and they were all either Immunes, or their bonded soulmates.

Sam

I'D BEEN PACING for the almost three hours since Molly had disappeared into what I'd decided must be a gateway to somewhere. I was seriously considering trying to enter the damn thing myself if she didn't come out soon. Because sometime during those three hours, I'd realised just how much I didn't want to live in a world without Molly.

She was everything I hadn't known was missing in my life. It was like I'd just been treading water waiting for her to come and teach me how to swim. Since she'd come into my life, I woke up every day looking forward to the time I got to spend with her. Magical bells and whistles, I was head-over-heels in love with this girl I'd only just met. So, the only question left then, was how *she* felt about *me*?

I wasn't stupid. I knew there was a spark between us, that she was drawn to me like I was to her. But was it strong enough to break the connection she'd already developed with Tray? I hadn't missed the increased number of glances Sarah and Tray had been throwing each other, and I hoped and prayed that meant what I thought it might. Were they developing feelings for each other? I closed my eyes and shook my head, determined to clear away all the thoughts racing around inside. It didn't matter who felt what for whom right then, because Molly was gone, and might never be coming back.

"Molly!" Sarah screamed, and I opened my eyes to see that Molly lay on a bed of leaves directly in front of the gateway. And then, before I could even stand up to run to Molly, the magical light blinked out of existence.

Okay, it looked like Sarah had been right, and it had only been there waiting for Molly.

But I didn't care about the hows or whys or anything else because Molly was back. I threw myself down on the ground beside her and lifted her into my lap. "Molly… sweetheart… are you okay?" I whispered into her ear.

Molly opened her eyes, and they widened at how close I was. Then she threw her arms around my neck and hung on for dear life. I looked up to see Tray and Sarah watching us with a smile on their faces. *Okay, so these were all good signs... weren't they?*

"I'm fine. But you are not going to believe any of what just happened. I don't even know where to start trying to explain it," Molly said, her voice muffled from where she had her face buried against my chest.

"How about we all just try to 'be' for a minute before you do that," I said, running my hands through the back of her hair. "We've all been worried sick, and it might take a minute to register that you're back and you're fine."

"I tried to tell them both that you'd be back as soon as you'd learned whatever the magic thing needed to tell you," Sarah said, hands on hips while she tapped her foot. All while wearing a huge grin. "But would they listen to me… noooo. What would Sarah—"

I nearly choked when Tray reached over and put his hand over Sarah's mouth. "I think we all got the message, Sar. You were right… we were wrong. Feel better now?"

She nodded and then licked Tray's palm. "Ewww… that is just gross."

"Well, next time, you might think twice about doing something so stupid. Or maybe, if there is a next time, I'll just bite you. This mouth has many hidden talents."

"I'm sure it has," Tray replied with a wicked grin, wiggling his eyebrows.

A shocked silence followed, and then everyone laughed. It seemed my sister may have finally met her match. So did that mean I might have a chance with Molly after all?

CHAPTER THIRTY-TWO

Sarah

"Fine," I said, struggling to keep my impatience in check. "But as soon as we're finished with the tents, we are all sitting down with a coffee while you tell us everything. Otherwise, I may just burst, and that wouldn't be pretty."

Molly just put her hand on her heart and grinned. "I promise," she said, and I nodded and went to help the boys.

We figured there were only a few hours left until darkness fell, so we'd decided to stay where we were already half set up and get an early start in the morning. Both tents were almost done, so I got busy putting our stuff inside and pulling out whatever bedding Harry had deemed necessary.

"Tents are done," Sam called out, "so I'll get the

coffee going." I tried not to giggle at the image of Sam and Tray planning who'd do what.

"Anything I can do to help, Sarah? Or does that *clever mouth* have everything under control?" Tray called out the same as Sam had. *Bloody smartarse!*

"I'll deal with you later," I muttered, continuing to pull stuff from the backpack. Maybe it could be Tray's job to try and fit it all *back into* the backpacks.

The sound of his low, sexy chuckle did funny things to my insides. Tray had been way more attentive since our little chat in the van, and I was getting more hopeful every minute that I might have a chance with him. I mean, it had been pretty obvious where Molly's affections lay when she threw herself on Sam the minute she opened her eyes. That had to mean something...right?

Sick to death of all the back and forth between them all, I decided that enough was enough. As soon as Molly finished telling them what had happened during the three hours she'd been gone, I was going to insist we review Sam's *no romantic feelings* rule and get everything out in the open. For magic's sake. We were adults, not children playing house.

Feeling much better after making my decision, I threw the bedding for the other tent inside it and moved to where the other three sat, all holding a coffee mug. Sam nodded to a spot next to the fire where another mug sat, and I grabbed it and joined them. Molly passed me the milk and sugar with a smile.

"So… thanks for giving me time to get everything I learned straight in my head. I think I know the best place to start now, but please don't expect to believe anything I tell you. Unfortunately, I can't use the same means as they did to prove what I'm saying is real."

What the hell was Molly talking about? She sounded tired, and scared and, well, just, overwhelmed. Before I could ask anything else, Molly started to speak.

When she started by telling us that she believed she'd been *'inside magic itself* with *the Source of all magic',* I didn't know whether to laugh, cry or run away screaming. Because wherever she'd been and whoever she'd been with, she'd obviously lost touch with reality. I looked around and caught the concerned looks on Sam and Tray's faces and knew they felt the same. *Our* Molly may be gone after all.

"Look, I can see from your faces that you think I've lost the plot. Hell, I thought someone had fed me hallucinogens, but you need to hear me out. Trust me, I wish *none* of it were true. But the magic *showed* me the proof inside my own head."

I wanted to kick myself for allowing my thoughts to show on my face so easily. Molly had obviously been through something traumatic, and the least we could do was listen with an open mind.

"Sorry Moll. Please, just keep going," Sam said, reaching for her hand and linking it with his. She gave him a grateful smile and then launched into the whole story. It didn't take long to realise that what Molly was saying was *not* something anyone could make up. The entire story sounded way too impossible, and at the same time plausible, to not be true.

"Oh, and just in case you were wondering, the three of you apparently have important parts to play in the battle ahead, too. Or at least that's what the Source said." She shrugged and seemed to slump into herself. Sam was behind her in an instant, letting her lean against him. No one said anything for a while. We were all too busy absorbing everything Molly had said.

"Well… that sucks!" I said—because it seemed an appropriate reaction. Molly had just gone from being a very small fish in a very large pond to the biggest fish ever born. And Immunes needed to guard her with our own lives. At least, that's how I'd interpreted what she'd said. It was kinda cool, in a way, knowing we were born to be so much more than what we'd been led to believe. Because if some of those Guardians had been soulmates with an Immune, then I was positive that was what was between Tray and me.

"It's probably not the ideal time for me to raise this issue, but after hearing that stuff about soulmates, I really need to get some things sorted out. So here goes: Molly, I love you like my own sister, but I think Sarah might be my soulmate."

I sat in stunned silence as Tray declared the words I'd been too afraid to hope for. I jumped up and threw myself into his lap, laughing and crying until Tray once again silenced me. But this time, he didn't use his hand.

Every nerve ending in my body sizzled when Tray's lips met mine. They were soft, and the pressure light and gentle. But the sound of the hallelujah chorus playing inside my head—something I'd never experienced when kissing anyone else—told me that Tray's assumption had been right. We were indeed soulmates, which made me a Guardian too!

I wanted to cry when Tray didn't deepen the kiss, but instead pulled away. *Later, beautiful.* His lips formed the words before he lifted his head, and my heart skipped a beat.

Bloody hell. I'd totally forgotten that Sam and Molly were sitting right next to us. I turned my head to apologise for our rude behaviour and grinned when I saw Sam and Molly engaged in a similar lip-lock to what I'd just experienced. I lifted my eyes to Tray's clear blue ones, starting to tingle all over again at the look in them. "I think it's safe to say that Molly and Sam don't have a problem with what you just said," I whispered, and then Tray lowered his head again and took up where we'd left off. And I melted into the euphoric bliss I'd never even known existed.

Molly

I HELD my breath when Sam reached around from behind me, lifted my chin and turned me to face him. The instant our eyes met, I felt the same connection that had confused me back in Sarah's tent at the opal mine. But this time, I allowed myself to fall into it, acknowledging the feeling of home he represented. Sam was everything, and I could finally let him in.

As soon as his lips closed over mine, my very soul seemed to vibrate with happiness. This was what I'd been waiting for. It wasn't just a kiss, it was as if our hearts, souls and minds merged, creating a bond I could swear I felt snapping into place. Before I was ready, Sam gently lifted his lips from mine, the intensity in his hazel eyes making my stomach do backflips. He rested his forehead against mine, his smile somehow brighter than I'd ever seen it before. *Damn, he was hot.*

"I don't know about you, but I'd much rather continue this without an audience," Sam whispered. Shit, I'd forgotten all about Tray and Sarah sitting beside us. Not that they looked like they cared where they were, they were as wrapped up in each other as Sam and I had been.

"Ahem," Sam said, and Molly had to giggle at how quickly Sarah and Tray pulled apart. "Sooo… that happened. Now what?" We all burst out laughing at Sam's concise summation of the situation. Yep, my man had a real skill with diplomacy. Still, he'd certainly eradicated all traces of any uncomfortable tension in the air.

"Can I assume the rule about romantic feelings is gone for good?" Sarah asked, a cheeky grin on her beautiful face.

"Hell yeah," Tray said, squeezing Sarah like a rag doll. "You can feel free to show as much of those romantic feelings as you like, gorgeous girl."

I was surprised to see Sarah's face turn bright pink. Wow, I'd never seen Sarah blush. In fact, I'd started to think that nothing embarrassed my resilient little friend. Who knew that all it would take was a term of endearment from Tray?

"So, I was thinking," Sam said, back to running his hand through my hair. The tender gesture had almost made me cry the last time he'd done it. But now? The last thing I wanted to do was cry. My body was on *fire*. I needed to be alone with Sam, just for a little while at least. As if he'd read my mind, Sam's next words had my head spinning.

"After everything that's happened today, I'd be happy to retire to my tent early and maybe share a meal with someone I'd like to get to know a little better. How do you all feel about that plan?"

A chorus of *yep, excellent idea,* and a *hell yeah* were the only answers he got as we all scrambled to get up and grab whatever food we wanted to take to our tents.

"Wait," Sam said, as we all headed for the tents. "I

just need to clarify something first. Tray, I know we were supposed to share a tent, but you *do* get that it was Molly I was talking about sharing a meal with. Right?" Sam ducked as everyone threw something they'd been holding at his head. He dived into the tent, laughing like a dying hyena, as we all parted ways for the rest of the evening.

CHAPTER THIRTY-THREE

Sam

Spending the night alone with Molly had been the greatest experience of my life. We'd talked, laughed and kissed for hours, discovering we had so much more in common than we ever could have guessed. And when we were so tired we couldn't keep our eyes open any longer, we'd snuggled down, and I'd slept with Molly wrapped in my arms. *Best. Night. Ever.*

"Okay, I have to ask. You'll probably think I'm crazy, but can you all see the faint glowing line stretching out in front of us?" Molly's words pulled me from my thoughts of the previous night, and I squeezed the hand I had tightly gripped in mine.

"Ummm… where should we be looking exactly? Is it on the ground or in the air in front of us?" I asked softly. The look of disappointment on her face had me desperately wishing I could see what she'd described.

"Never mind, "she said with a sad sigh. "But if I'm seeing it, do you think it might be something the Source left for us to follow? They certainly had a vested interest in us finding Zion."

Sarah and Tray, who'd fallen back so we could all enjoy a little bit more alone time, were suddenly right beside us. "I don't think it matters whether anyone else can see it or not," Sarah said. "If you're seeing it, Molly, then we should definitely follow it. I mean, what have we got to lose? It's not like we have any idea where we're going."

"Yep. What she said," Tray interjected, and we all chuckled. I'd noticed that everyone's mood had lifted since our change in circumstances. Seemed that not having to fight an attraction to the one you were meant to be with made the world a much better place. Even if our other circumstances left a lot to be desired.

"But why am I the only one who can see it? You all saw the magic strands that came out of the gateway before I was sucked inside, didn't you?" We all nodded, and Molly huffed. "Then why can't you see this line?"

I was surprised when Tray reached out to touch Molly's shoulder. "Hey, huni, something tells me this won't be the only time something like this happens. The Source wouldn't want to risk anyone seeing the line who shouldn't, so that just means we need to trust and follow you. Another thing I think you should start getting used to."

Molly's beautiful eyes were glassy with unshed tears as she looked around at the three of us. "But what if I don't want—"

I pulled her into my arms just as the first tears began to leak from her eyes. "I'm so sorry, baby, but I think the choice has been taken out of your hands. This is what you were born to do, and we all know you can't fight destiny. But... even though we don't see the trail, or whatever other signs the Source sends you, we'll be there with you all the way."

"What he said..." chirped Sarah.

"Absolutely," Tray said.

"See... we're family, remember. And yeah, I know what you're all gonna say, but we *are* still family. Just a slightly different family than we were yesterday."

Relief flooded through me as I felt Molly's shoulders shake beneath my hands. Even my sense of humour and ability to make others laugh had improved since finding Molly. *Who knew, eh?*

A howl of pain shattered the silence around us, the sound emanating from somewhere behind us and to the right. Then, the boom from what had to be a blast of magic made the earth shake. *What the hell?*

Molly lifted her head and looked behind us, then looked ahead and to the left. "Quick, the magic path just shifted, and I'm thinking now is a good time to follow it."

Nobody argued as we followed Molly along the path only she could see. I held her hand tight, trying to send reassurance through our link. We thrashed through the bush, and I hoped whoever was behind us was too occupied with whatever had happened to hear our movements.

"Wait…" Molly said, stopping abruptly. "The magic is glowing really bright and pulsing just up ahead. It feels like a warning or something. What do we do?"

"Is it suggesting an alternate path?" Tray asked over Molly's shoulder.

Molly shook her head. "Nope, it's like we need to keep going that way, but there's some form of obstacle."

I scratched my head and shared a look with Sarah. It was like we were each trying to tell the other one that we'd handle it. But before we could agree, Tray had moved to where a large rock sat, hefted it into his arms, and hurled it onto the path ahead of us. As soon as the rock hit the ground, a huge crater opened up beneath it, and the rock hurtled downwards.

"Woah," Tray said. "Lucky I went with Plan B, eh?"

"Why?" Sarah asked, eyebrow raised. "What was Plan A?"

"I think it might be best for everyone if I kept that information to myself." Sarah punched his arm, and then we all turned to inspect the results of the disaster we'd averted.

"Where's the path going now, baby?" I asked softly, wrapping my arm around Molly's shaking body.

She looked up into my eyes, and I saw the horror reflected in them. "Shit, Sam, if we… I mean that could've…"

"Hey, it's okay. It didn't happen, and that's all that matters. Now, where does the path go next? Because we still have someone behind us who obviously didn't fare as well as us with whatever booby-trap they encountered."

Molly

I WAS SERIOUSLY STARTING to feel like I was falling apart at the seams. For magic's sake! Could I just get five minutes to pull myself together and try to get my head around everything that had happened in the last twenty-four hours? I needed to stop feeling and acting like the victim and make a concerted effort to step up and accept what fate had handed me. No more of the simpering idiot who reacted to everything like a Nothing. That Molly was gone for good. And even though I didn't know who or what I was, the Source had told me I was Something.

So… I wasn't a Magic, I wasn't an Immune, and I definitely was not a Nothing. I was some kind of hotch-potch blend of all three. *Great... once again I was just a different form of freak.* Except that apparently, this time, I was an important one. Oh, and I was *personally responsible for repairing the very fabric of the world. Huh... no pressure...right?*

Which is when I started to laugh. Yep, I sat down on the ground in front of the huge crater and laughed until the tears rolled down my face. Sam tried to reach for me, but I just held up my hand, shook my head, and continued to laugh. I knew I was on the verge of hysteria, and by the looks on my friends' faces, they knew it too. But I needed to do this. It was like I was purging all the fear and confusion and denial that had been raging through me since this whole thing began. I shut out everyone and everything around me and just let go. And it was working.

When I finally got myself back under control, I noticed that my friends sat around me in a circle, their worried faces watching me like hawks. I sucked in a couple of deep breaths and tried to summon a smile. "Yeah, sorry about that," I said, looking down at my hands. "I just... it all just..."

"Hey, you don't need to apologise. I'm amazed that you made it this far without all the crap that's been thrown at you sending you off the deep end," Sarah said, patting my hand.

"But you're all coping—" I said, before Sam squeezed my other hand.

"Hey, we've all got a much easier job than you,

sweetheart. We only need to trust and follow you. Remember what you said to me about being a leader when I said I didn't want it? *Hmmm...?*"

Damn him. Why did he have to have such a good memory? "Yeah, yeah, smartarse. I remember. Something about *you can't just not step up because you don't feel like it.*"

Sam gave me a smug grin, and I punched his shoulder. "Fine. I'm working on it, okay? It might just take me a bit longer than five minutes to get on board with this whole *leader* thing. It's not like I've had any experience in the role."

"Oh, I don't know," Tray piped in, rubbing his chin. "I seem to recall more than a few times you were a bossy—" Sarah and I both punched him at the same time, and we all chuckled. Well, except Tray, who was rubbing his shoulders and looking like a petulant child who felt he'd been unjustly punished.

CHAPTER THIRTY-FOUR

Tray

I rubbed my poor old shoulders and chuckled to myself as we all stood and brushed ourselves off. I'd been really worried about Molly's mental health for a while there, and the price of a couple of sore shoulders was worth seeing her smile again.

"I'm not sure what we're supposed to do here," Molly said, pulling her hair out and redoing it in a messy bun. "The path literally starts again on the other side of the crater. Does anyone have any suggestions for how we can magically or otherwise transport to the other side?"

"What about if we built some kind of bridge across?" Sarah suggested, looking around as she spoke.

There must be at least one tree around here tall enough to reach the other side. Look, how about that one? I could just zap it, and it would fall pretty much exactly where we need it."

Sam shook his head. "I don't think using magic would be a very good idea right now. Remember how we heard the ones following us using it?"

"Wait. I'm sure I saw rope in one of the backpacks," I said. "What if we tie a rope to that tree and use it to swing across?" I didn't miss the way the girls' faces turned a sickly shade of white. "Or not?"

"Hang on," Sam put in, a twinkle of excitement in his eyes. "How about I swing across and secure it at the other side? Then it would be like ziplining across. Way easier for the girls."

The grateful look he received from Molly and Sarah told me he'd picked a winner. But I wasn't about to let Sam have all the glory without a fight. I knew the grin I wore held a challenge Sam wouldn't be able to resist. "In the name of fairness for all, I reckon we should *scissors, paper, rock* for who gets to swing across. You can't have it all your way all the time, man. Besides, the loser has to climb the tree to tie the rope on."

"Absolutely," Sam said with a grin similar to mine. "Bring it on."

The outcome was better than I'd hoped and expected. Sam won the first one, I won the second and then I won the third as well. "Woohoo," I cried, doing a happy dance. "I've never climbed a tree in my life, and I wasn't looking forward to that one being my first. I grew up in the city, remember?"

"So, what about the rope swinging? Have you done that before?" Sam asked, a concerned frown on his face.

"Now *that* I've done before. Don't you go worrying about me, bro. You'd best get started on the tree-climbing part of this plan."

"Please be careful," Molly said, grabbing Sam's arm before he could dig out the rope from the backpack.

"It's okay, baby. Unlike some other people, I've climbed trees, fences—you name it, I've climbed it. Climbing is a necessary skill for someone on the run. Maybe I could give Tray a few lessons when we're not quite so busy."

"Yeah, yeah. Be the hero," I said with a smirk. Then I pulled the rope from the backpack and handed it to him. "But at least I don't have to climb *that* tree."

"Whatever," Sam said as he threw the rope over his shoulder and headed toward the massive tree to the side of the path.

I watched in awe as Sam scaled the tree like a damned monkey. Why did he have to always be so much better at stuff than me? Sarah's arm slid around my waist, and I knew she must have seen the envy on my face. "Everyone has strengths and weaknesses in certain areas. Sam's skills have been honed by being on the run for years. I'm sure we'll need one of your strengths before this is all over."

I leaned down and kissed her forehead, knowing

that I finally had my *'person'*. I always remembered Mum and Dad saying they were each other's *person*, and I finally understood what they'd meant.

"Is this branch high enough, do you reckon? It stretches a good way over the crater and seems to be sturdy enough." Sam's voice drifted down from above, and we all looked up to see where he was. Then we all looked at each other and nodded. "Yep, looks perfect," I yelled back, and he started to shuffle forward onto the branch. When he reached a spot that appeared to stretch about halfway across the crater below it, he began to tie off the rope.

"Are you sure you're okay to do the rope swing? Because I could always give it—" I kissed Sarah before she could finish offering to do my job. She was amazing and could probably do it with one arm tied behind her back. But I needed to feel like I was pulling my weight. It wasn't like I brought a truckload of skills to the table. Besides, the kiss was everything I hadn't known I'd needed right then, and I felt seven feet tall and bullet-proof already.

Sam was already scrambling back down the tree by the time I lifted my head from Sarah's. He'd tied the end of the rope around his wrist—a good way to make sure he didn't drop it on his way back down.

"Okay, Tarzan. You're up," Sam said, handing me the end of the rope. "So, there's only one thing wrong with our plan. If we go with the zipline idea, the girls will have to climb the tree to get started." He turned to Sarah and me. "Are you sure you wouldn't rather swing over? Tray will be there to grab you on the other side if you need help."

Sarah and Molly looked up at the tree at the same time, then swung their eyes over to where the crater ended. It was about ten feet across. Then they looked at each other and both said *'swing'* at exactly the same time. We all laughed and began searching for anything that could act as gloves for gripping the rope. Sam let out a hoot and held up what looked to be four pairs of gloves in a plastic bag.

"I love Harry," Sarah sighed.

"I saw him first," Molly quipped with a wink at Sam.

Sarah

I TRIED to quell the nerves making me want to throw up as I held the newly returned rope in my hand. Tray, Sam and Molly all now stood on the other side of the crater, calling out encouraging words as I stood frozen where I was. *Why the hell had I insisted on going last?* Because I was a stubborn cow who'd wanted to delay the inevitable for as long as possible. *Seriously? Did I have to always end up being the dumbarse?*

I had just sucked in a breath ready to take off when I heard the voices. I held a finger in front of my lips and shook my head to let the others know not to call out.

"I'm telling you, the voices are coming from over in that direction," the first voice said.

"Like we'd listen to you after the last trap you led us into. We'll catch up to them, as long as we keep moving forward. They're only kids, for magic's sake, with not a lick of magic between them. The Council were very clear in their instructions. They are not to leave here alive."

"But they're Immunes, so our magic—"

"Won't work anywhere near as well as these guns. Now shut up and keep moving."

My entire body was shaking now. But not with fear. I was so angry I wanted to wait for whoever was coming and blast them with my *not a lick of magic.* These Magic Councillors, or whoever the hell they were, were planning to just… shoot us. But no matter how tempting it was to prove them wrong, I knew I needed to get to the other side and tell the others what I'd heard. Without another thought, I sucked in a breath, got a good grip on the rope, and leapt off the edge, just as I'd watched the others do before me.

I hadn't realised I'd closed my eyes until I felt a pair

of warm, strong arms wrap around me, and a whisper that I could let go. I sagged into Tray's arms and decided I would definitely be living right there from now on.

"What the hell happened, Sar?" Sam asked, and I snapped out of my daze.

"I'll tell you later. Right now, we need to get as far from here as possible. Is there any way to remove, or at least hide the rope?"

Sam looked up at the rope and shook his head. "Do we have enough time for me to climb—"

Unbelievable! Why the hell hadn't I thought to use my magic earlier. I slapped my forehead—mainly because I felt somebody needed to—then pointed at the top of the rope and flicked my wrist. The rope detached itself and fell into the crater. "I have magic, remember? I can't believe I didn't think of doing that instead of you having to climb that tree. Seriously, I think my brain needs a major reboot."

"That's okay sis. I'll forgive you just this once. Mainly because none of us thought of using your magic either," Sam gave me a cheeky grin.

"Hey, that's right. You're all as bad as me. Okay, enough talk. Molly, you're up. Get us the hell outta here, sister," I said, and then we were practically running as we followed Molly through the dense bush.

Twenty minutes later, I felt like my heart would jump out of my chest if we didn't stop for a minute. I heard Molly's gasp from in front of me and looked up to see what was wrong. The mouth of a cave loomed in front of us, and from the way Molly was acting, I guessed the magical path must have led directly inside it.

Oh yeah. Just another claustrophobic's worst nightmare.

CHAPTER THIRTY-FIVE

Sam

I knew from the look of abject horror on Molly's face that the magic path led directly into the dark cavernous maw of the cave in front of us. A magic-be-damned, horror-filled repeat of her experience at the mine. This was total and utter bullshit. Wrapping my arms around her I turned her face away from the sight her eyes had been riveted to.

"Hey baby," I said, lifting her chin until her eyes met mine. "We don't have to—"

"I know you're only trying to make me feel better, and I love that you'd even *try* to find a way around this. But we both know there's no other way. Either I go inside that cave, or we never make it to Zion. And that's not an option I'd ever consider after my time with the Source. We have to make it to Zion. So we *will* be going inside that cave."

I waited for the tears or any other signs of terror she'd exhibited previously, but there was nothing. Just a look of determination in her eyes I hadn't seen before. "Wow. Where did this Molly come from?" I asked, searching her eyes for any sign of the old Molly.

Molly just shrugged and smiled. "Yeah, she came along when I was in the middle of the hysterical laughter session earlier. She had some pretty interesting stuff to say about not being weak anymore, so I invited her to join us. What do you think so far? Think she'll fit in okay?"

I answered her with a kiss. I still couldn't believe this beautiful, strong, feisty woman had chosen me as her partner. That she'd ever doubted herself enough to feel she needed to adopt a stronger version of herself made my heart ache. But if it helped her to deal with the battles I knew we had ahead of us, then I was glad she'd found a way to strengthen herself.

"Ummm… should we be worried about what's happening there?" Sarah asked as the ground began to vibrate. I looked up to find the entrance to the cave closing before our eyes. That couldn't be good.

When the entrance was completely sealed, what looked a lot like words began to appear on the rock face where the opening had been. I looked around at the others and was relieved to see that they were all staring at the same spot.

"Wait… are they words?" Tray asked, his voice holding a nervous waver. "And are they seriously being burned into the rock while we watch?"

"Glad I'm not the only one seeing that," I said, as Molly tried to remove herself from my embrace. "Don't even think about it, Moll. At least wait until the writing stops… please."

She nodded, and I pulled her back against my front so we could watch the scene unfolding before us. "Hey," I whispered into her ear. "Maybe this means we won't have to go in there after all."

"I can't decide whether you're the world's greatest optimist or just an idiot trying to make me feel better," she replied, never taking her eyes from where the words continued to appear.

"Maybe a bit of both," I said, kissing her ear and grinning at the shiver she couldn't hide.

"I think it's done," said Sarah, who now stood the closest to where the words had appeared. "It looks like four lines of text. It's been a while since any new words appeared. Can we puh-lease move close enough to see what it says before I burst?"

"Listen here wildcat! Haven't you ever heard the saying *curiosity killed the cat?*" Tray asked as he stopped her from moving forward.

"Yeah, but the thing is… if I'm a cat, I have nine lives. Sooo… I can afford to lose a few." Sarah shrugged and threw me an imploring look. "Which means I'm the best person to risk getting closer."

All I could do was shake my head. It was Molly who finally answered her. "Fine. But I'm warning you… if you die, I'll wait for you to come back and take the next life myself. Now please… be careful."

Sarah glared at Tray until he let her hand go and then strutted over to stand in front of the words. "It's a rhyme with what I think is some kind of cryptic message," she said as she read. "Want me to read it out, or are you all feeling brave enough to come closer now I didn't explode or something equally gross… and messy?"

Molly had stepped forward out of my arms and was beside Sarah before I could even blink. "Oh cool, the writing looks ancient. Do you guys wanna come over, or should one of us read it out?"

"Oh, for magic's sake. Can one of you just read it out loud so we know what we have to do? You seem to forget people are chasing us," Sam said, folding his arms across his chest and staying where he was.

ENTER THOSE WHO FEEL THEY MUST
    YOUR ANSWERS LIE BENEATH THE DUST
    BUT HEED YE WELL, FOR YE MAY SEE
    YOURSELF, OR HOW THAT SELF SHOULD BE

THE WORDS HUNG in the air after Sarah finished reciting them. No one spoke, as if we were all busy pondering the meaning of the cryptic words. Well, at least we knew the message applied to us. After all, Molly had been told by the Source that we *must* get to Zion.

"So, the thing is—we could stand around here all day trying to figure out what the damn message means, but that won't change the fact that we need to go in. Regardless of what we might find. Am I right?" Tray had adopted the exact same stance as me and had also directed that last question at me.

I nodded and shrugged. "Okay, genius. I agree. But how the hell do we get the door to open?"

A flame appeared to burst from the wall and Molly and Sarah jumped back in shock. An instant later, the flame was gone, and a new line appeared under the other four. The words blazed as they grew larger, until Tray and I could read them from where we stood.

"You were saying…" Tray said, reading the new words aloud:

ONLY BLOOD WILL BREAK THE SEAL

"JUST EWWW. The damned rock wants blood? That is just gross," Sarah said in disgust. "And how do we even know *whose* blood it wants?"

"Yeah, yeah. We all know it's mine it wants," Molly

said, looking at me. "Looks like we've found a use for one of those knives Harry packed for us."

"Molly… there's no way—" I spluttered, horrified at the thought of Molly having to use her blood to get us inside.

"Don't Sam, please," Molly said, jumping in before I could finish what I wanted to say. "I really appreciate you trying to protect me, but you need to accept that from here on in, there'll be stuff I just have to do. Just promise me you'll be there to pick up the pieces *after* I've done what's needed?"

I stared at Molly for a long time. She really had changed. I knew she'd had to embrace the change in order to do what she was born to do. But I wanted to be beside her when she took on whatever trials were ahead. Not waiting in the background while she faced them alone.

I loved this girl with every fibre of my being. Finally acknowledging the fact, even if it was only to myself, was the most freeing experience of my life. Yes, I loved her… and I had no desire whatsoever to live without her.

"Okay, I'll make a deal with you. I'll agree to stop being overprotective—if you do, too." I put my hand up before Molly's confused look could transform into a demand for answers. "Now it's your turn to accept that you won't be doing it all on your own with me waiting in the wings. I want to be *beside* you every step of the way. We're a team, damnit, so stop trying to push me away. I love you, Molly Chambers, so just… *well, deal with it.*"

I looked down at the dirt beneath our feet and scuffed the toe of my boot like a little kid who'd said too much. I hadn't meant to say that last bit, but it had slipped out anyway. I waited for Molly to tell me to take a hike, but instead, she threw her arms around me and kissed me until my knees were ready to buckle.

"Thank you, Sam," she said when she finally allowed our lips to part. "You didn't have to say—"

I put a finger in front of her lips. "Don't you dare try to downplay what I just said. *I. Love. You. Molly Chambers.* It doesn't matter if you don't feel the same way. I'm already the happiest I've ever been in my entire life."

CHAPTER THIRTY-SIX

Molly

Sam loved me. Like, absolutely, positively loved me. But I couldn't say the words back because I hadn't even had the time or energy to analyse my feelings for him. I mean, I liked him. Okay, I *really* liked him. But with everything else going on around us, I couldn't focus enough of my energy to decide whether I did or didn't *love* him.

"Ahem," Sarah's voice penetrated the daze I'd been in, and I looked around in confusion. Shit, I'd forgotten Sarah and Tray were even here, let alone within hearing distance for our little melodrama. "Sorry to interrupt, but we seriously need to get moving. Because I do not want to be standing here when those guns turn up."

I looked back to find Sam had one of the knives in

his hand, and he reached for my hand with his other one. "Together?" he asked softly.

I smiled and nodded as I took his hand, and he led us to a spot right in front of the newly burned words. "Ready?" Sam's voice was even softer than the last time he'd spoken. He lifted our joined hands, separated them, and then made a small incision in the palm of my hand. I flinched, but it was only a small sting. Then I watched in awe as Sam did the same to his own hand.

"You are not doing this alone. They can either have both of our blood, or none," Sam said, a little louder than before. Then we both placed our palms against the rock, just below the word blood. Nothing happened for a few seconds, and then the rock began to vibrate beneath our hands, and Sam pulled us back. In less than a minute, the gaping maw was back in front of us.

I looked around at my friends and tried to put on a brave smile. "Well, what are we waiting for? Putting it off won't make it any easier." Inside, my stomach felt like it had been invaded by a horde of angry bees, and the claustrophobia-induced fear seemed to join them in gnawing at my stomach walls.

"We need to stay together," Sam said, the nerves he was trying to hide making his voice waver slightly. "No matter what happens, don't let go of the hand of whoever is next to you. I'll go first, then Molly, then Sarah, and then Tray can bring up the rear. Everybody good to go?"

We all nodded and followed Sam into the cave.

The maelstrom of wind that hit us as soon as Tray had stepped across the threshold tore my hands from my friends and then I was flying and tumbling through the air, headed for who knew where. I was so dizzy I had to fight back the nausea. The thought of vomit tumbling around with me helped to hold it at bay. Just when I felt ready to pass out, something hit me from above, and the world went even blacker than it had already been.

Sarah

I WOKE up to the usual sounds of people bustling past my tent. My head was sore, and I couldn't remember what could have happened the previous night to make it ache this much. Well, it was probably self-induced, so no use complaining.

I quickly pulled on my clothes and crossed to the other side of the mine to grab a much-needed coffee. It was nice to be home.

Wait, where had that thought come from? That was something you thought after you'd returned from being away from home, and I hadn't been anywhere. *Had I?*

"Hey Sarah," Mike said, shoving his butt along the bench seat to make room for me. "You're looking a bit worse for wear this morning. What were you up to last night?"

"I was hoping maybe you could tell me that," I said, sipping on the delicious hot brew in my hand. "I have no recollection of anything from last night."

"Sorry, I didn't see you around. Thought you must have decided to have an early night."

Okay, so where the hell was I last night? I tried to recall any of the details from the previous day, but all I found was a blank void. Hmmm… maybe Sam would be able to tell me why everything felt so weird.

I sat sipping on my coffee and was suddenly hit by the thought that I couldn't remember the last time I'd had one. Oh well, I wasn't going to waste this one. Sam could wait.

I listened to the laughter and chatter around me, but I couldn't relax. I was plagued by the thought that there was something important I needed to do. Looking around at my friends, and the place where I'd been the happiest in years, I couldn't work out why it felt like it wasn't enough.

What was I missing? The urge to find Sam had become an overwhelming need, and I swung my legs around to leave the table.

Mike's big arm was around my shoulders before I

could move. "What's goin' on, Sarah? You're actin' like a caged animal."

"What? Why would I be looking like that?"

"I don't know, huni. But you do."

"I'm okay. I just need to speak to Sam."

"Who?"

I rolled my eyes. "Sam… you know, my *twin brother?* The one who kicks your butt on the regular?"

Mike seemed to be studying me, as if worried I'd lost my mind. Shit, maybe I had. Because nothing around here was making any sense. Mike hadn't answered my question about Sam, but the look in his eyes was starting to scare me. "Sorry Mike, I'm a bit off this morning. I might just go back to bed for a while."

I scrambled out from under his arm and launched off the bench seat. Then I ran as fast as my feet would carry me to Sam's tent. When I reached the spot where it should have been, it wasn't there. What the…?

The memories slammed into me like a wrecking ball. None of this was real! Sam was back in the cave, with Tray and Molly. Oh fates, I needed to get back to them. Before I could blink, the wind that I only now remembered had been responsible for putting me where I was, swept me up into the air and everything went black… *again.*

Tray

I WOKE to what felt like an elephant jumping on my chest. Okay, so maybe *elephant* was a slight exaggeration. Besides, I'd never heard of an elephant giggling.

"Come on sleepyhead, breakfast is ready. Mum said if you're not downstairs in two minutes, she'd throw yours in the bin." Emily tried to wriggle her way off the bed, but I caught her and planted a big wet kiss on her forehead.

"Yuck. Keep your stupid boy germs to yourself," she said, finally making it off the bed. "Better hurry..." she called as she ran off down the hallway. Damn, I'd missed her.

Sorry? And why would I have missed her? I only saw her last night... didn't I? Although, for the life of me I couldn't remember anything about last night. Wait, I couldn't even remember the entire previous day. What the hell was wrong with me?

"*Tra-ay,*" my mum's voice floated up from the kitchen. "That's one minute gone already." Pushing aside all thoughts of the lost memories, I dived out of bed, pulled on the clothes from the floor, and took the stairs two at a time.

"I'm here. I'm here. Leave that food right where it is, thank you very much," I said as I hurried into the kitchen and sat down in front of a huge stack of pancakes. Nothing in the world tasted as good as my mum's pancakes. I smiled at the sight of my dad sitting at the end of the table reading the paper. Everything was just like it used to be.

Used to be? Like, it hadn't changed, had it? Nope, I wasn't going to dwell on my mind's ridiculous thoughts for another minute. Breakfast as a family had always been my favourite part of the day. Usually, though, there'd be lots of chatter about what each of us had planned for the day. In fact, it was so quiet it felt weird. Something else was missing besides the conversation. What was it?

As if prompted by my thoughts, Mum and Dad began chatting about something totally boring and I dived into the pancake feast in front of me. "Mum," I said as I swallowed down another forkload. "You really need to cook these more often. I can't even remember the last time I had them."

Mum and Dad gave each other a funny look, and then Mum balled up the tea towel in her hand and threw it at my head. "Very funny. Now just eat so I can get the kitchen cleaned up."

"Hang on. What was so funny? I was serious about the pancakes."

"Tray, stop messing with your mother. You don't need to get smart-mouthed just because we've had them every day this week. Be grateful she's cooked you anything."

I looked from one to the other and realised they were deadly serious. *So why couldn't I remember the last time I'd had pancakes?* My appetite now gone, I excused myself and headed back to my room. Something was wrong. I could feel it in my bones. I was missing something.

I stumbled over something on the floor just as I was about to reach into the cupboard for some clean clothes. An unfamiliar and extremely dirty glove sat on the carpet, and I staggered as the memories flooded into my brain.

This wasn't where I was supposed to be. My friends needed me. Sarah... Then the wind was back. Which was the one thing I wished had stayed an unpleasant memory. Once again, I was lifted into the air and pummelled by the wind coming from every direction at once. Then, thankfully, the blackness took over, just as it had before.

CHAPTER THIRTY-SEVEN

Sam

I woke from the best sleep I could remember having in a very long time. The wind rustled the leaves of the tree outside my bedroom window and the sunshine played across the dappled carpet. The fact that I was mesmerised by a sight I witnessed pretty much every day at this time of year was weird. But hey, I'd woken in a fantastic mood, and maybe it was one of those days where you needed to just stop and smell the roses, so to speak.

I looked around the room, not sure what I was looking for, but knowing there should be something or someone here that wasn't. And it was important, damnit. I wracked my brain trying to remember what I was searching for and was freaked out to discover I had no memories of anything. Like, seriously, there were none. My mind reeled with questions.

How the hell had my memory been wiped?

What was so important that I needed to have no memory of it?

Who had wiped it?

And finally, why?

Nope, this was not happening. I could hear Sarah and my parents' voices coming from the kitchen and could smell the delicious aroma of bacon and eggs, not to mention coffee. But I was not leaving this room until I knew what was going on. I spotted my discarded clothes lying on the ground and jumped out of bed to grab them. Maybe there'd be some sign of where I'd been last night that would tell me where I'd been.

As I reached for my jeans, a slight sting on the palm of my hand pulled me up short. *Okay, this was getting ridiculous. How did I not even remember cutting myself?* Something was really wrong here. As soon as I touched the small cut, the memories flooded into me. Bloody magic's balls... Molly. And Sarah and Tray. Wait, how had I heard Sarah's voice in the kitchen? *A damned illusion! None of this was real.*

I needed to get back to Molly and the others. But I was stuck inside—the all too familiar wind I now remembered picking me up in the cave swept me up and tossed me around like a rag doll. Gritting my teeth, I tried to prepare myself for whatever happened next.

My last thought before the blackness overtook me was that I *would* be finding Molly sooner rather than later.

Molly

I OPENED my eyes and reached for the warm body I expected to find snuggled up behind me. *Wait... who was I expecting to find there?* I giggled at the thought that I must have had one hell of a good dream to make me think it was that real. Not that I could remember it, of course. *Damnit, I finally get some action, even if only in my imagination, and I can't remember one single detail. Typical!*

I lay in bed wondering why Mum hadn't called me down for breakfast. It was after 7 am and she wasn't hassling me. What was that about? Wait… maybe it was the weekend, and I didn't have school today. Yesssss, I hissed and punched the air.

I reached over to my bedside table and picked up the book I'd been hanging to read for ages. I wasn't really hungry, so I snuggled back down under the covers and immersed myself in a world of dragons and witches. This was my favourite thing to do on a weekend. It provided an escape from my sad, miserable world, and allowed me to push away all other thoughts and worries for a while.

"Molly," my mum's voice floated up from downstairs. "Last chance to come and grab some breakfast before I clear it all away."

I looked up at the clock on the wall and was surprised to find it was 9 am. *Wow. Where did that two hours go?*

"Hang on, I'm coming now," I called out as I stumbled out of bed and looked around for the clothes I'd worn the day before. They should be on the floor... that's where I always left them. But nope. Nothing there. I tried to think what I'd been wearing, in case I'd thrown them somewhere different, but the memory wasn't there. *Right. What the hell was that about?* Then an eerie feeling shuddered through me as I realised I had no memories whatsoever. I mean, I recognised everything around me, and my mum's voice that had just called from the kitchen. But I had no memory of what I'd done or where I'd been for... well... ever.

Sooo... I knew who and where I was right now. Like, my surroundings were familiar. So that ruled out amnesia. I felt all around my head for a lump or anything that might indicate I'd fallen down the stairs or something. Nope... nothing. So why couldn't I remember where I'd been or what I'd done? And why did I have this niggling feeling in the back of my mind that I'd forgotten something super important?

"Mum, where are my clothes from yesterday?" I yelled.

"I grabbed them earlier and they're in the wash. They reeked of fire and smoke. Why would—"

Mum's voice faded into the distance as her words settled over me. *Fire and smoke? Where the hell*—I sank to the floor as the memories began to trickle in. Sam. That was who I'd been expecting to find snuggled against me this morning. Tray, my newly discovered best friend, swinging across a giant chasm on a rope. And Sarah, her beautiful eyes shining with tears as we laughed together. How could I have forgotten them?

Because someone had taken me away, wiped my memories and deposited me in this make-believe world based on reality.

"Enough," I yelled to whoever was listening, and I knew there would be someone. "Whoever you are, you'd better get me back to my friends right now before I... well, before I do something we might all regret!"

The wind appeared out of nowhere and wrapped around my entire body, lifting me into the air. I almost laughed when I wasn't tossed around like I remembered being last time, as if that someone I'd yelled at knew not to push his luck.

Instead of the world going black like it had last time, I could see a large space ahead and below us. When we got closer, I could make out three people who appeared to be in the middle of a heated argument. Well, at least that *someone* had brought me to my friends.

As if he'd felt us drawing near, Sam looked up and the relief on his face made my heart swell. *This man* was who I'd been searching for in my bed earlier. Suddenly, I knew beyond a shadow of a doubt that I loved Sam more than life itself. I couldn't wait to be back on the ground so I could throw myself into his arms and tell him I was never letting go.

CHAPTER THIRTY-EIGHT

Tray

I pulled Sarah into my arms as we both tried not to watch Sam and Molly's reconciliation. But after the state Sam had been in for the last couple of hours, it was great to see him whole again. Not to mention how long Sarah and I had avoided touching each other.

Sam had been the first to arrive in the massive chamber carved out of the rock surrounding them. Apparently, he'd yelled and cursed for a while, swearing vengeance on those who'd separated him from Molly. By the time I'd arrived, he was practically hoarse from shouting. We sat together and compared stories, relieved to learn that our experiences had been almost identical.

When Sarah arrived, she was still groggy from the

sleep the wind seemed to be able to induce at will, and I cradled her in my arms until she was coherent once more.

"Where's Molly?" were the first words out of her mouth.

Sam cursed and turned away, resuming the pacing he'd been doing since we'd finished sharing our experiences. Sarah and I quickly compared stories, and I found it interesting that Sarah's experience wasn't at home. We decided it was because none of us had chosen to leave our homes and families, whereas Sarah had. The Immune Community had been her version of the place she hadn't chosen to leave.

"As you can see, Sam's a mess," I said, nodding toward where Sam paced and muttered curses. "We don't even know if Molly was placed in a similar experience to us. But if she was, why haven't her memories returned? Is she really just accepting that she's where she's supposed to be?"

"Nope, I don't believe that," Sarah said. "The fact that I couldn't remember the night before, or anything before that, had alarm bells going off in my head. Molly would be the same."

"But Sam reckons he's been here almost two hours. Surely, she's questioned something by now?"

Sarah stood and brushed herself off. "Shit, I don't have any answers either. What are we supposed to do? Sit here and wait for magic knows what 'til magic knows when? This is bloody ridiculous. But one thing I do know is that I need to speak to Sam. I don't think watching us comforting each other and knowing what he's missing is helping."

I groaned when I realised how insensitive Sarah and I had been. I'd been so relieved to see Sarah, I hadn't even considered how our reconciliation would affect Sam. Sarah must have noticed my look of regret, because she bent down and pressed a kiss against my lips. "Hey, it's okay. We might just need to curb the PDA for a while."

I nodded as I watched her walk to her brother and throw an arm over his shoulder. I'd been trying to hide my own distress over Molly's disappearance. Sure, we were both with someone else now, but Molly had become a blend of my best friend and my sister. And I was way more worried than I was letting on.

I thought about everything that had happened since we'd left Medulla, and I tried to put myself in Molly's shoes. If I'd learned what she had about herself, on top of the expectations placed upon her against her will, I'd probably grab the opportunity to walk away if it were presented to me. If she'd woken in her own bed, back in the world she'd been dragged away from, why wouldn't she choose to just brush the memories aside and stay where she was?

"We need to do something!" Sam yelled as he stalked toward where I sat, with Sarah trailing behind him. "You can't tell me that there's not someone running this entire show. Whoever it is, they are playing with our lives, and I've had enough."

"I agree, Sam," I said, holding up my hands to placate him. "But didn't you say you spent the first hour you were here yelling and swearing at whoever might be listening? The fact that you got no response tells me we probably won't get one now. So, what do you suggest we do?"

I didn't want to antagonise him any further, but walking around demanding that we take action wasn't helping anyone. Sam looked as if he were about to say something, and then he went very still. His head tipped back, and he squinted over my shoulder toward the other end of the chamber. The relief that spread across his face was a sight to behold. I spun, following his gaze, and couldn't believe I saw Molly being carried toward us by an unusually calm and controlled wind. A far cry from the way we'd been delivered.

"*Now* you can do the old PDA to your heart's content. Because I will definitely *not* be complaining if you do," Sarah whispered into my ear. Damn this woman and her sexy voice. She had the *sultry temptress* routine down to a fine art, and I spent way too much of my time imagining things I shouldn't. I wasn't sure whether I was relieved or disappointed when I heard Molly's voice.

"I'm really sorry you guys had to wait so long for me," Molly said, walking over to where we stood, Sam's hand firmly wrapped around hers. "I kinda stuffed up, and instead of pondering what was wrong, I buried myself in a book for two hours and shut the world out."

"Seriously?" Sarah said with a giggle. "You were reading a book this whole time. Must have been a good one."

"Yeah, it was great. Not that I'll ever get the chance to finish it now. So, what did I miss?"

You have missed nothing important, Little Saviour. I jumped as the voice seemed to come from everywhere at once. Fortunately, I still held Sarah in my arms, and I noticed Sam pulling Molly into his.

It is good that you have all passed. Now you may proceed to Zion.

"This was all just some stupid test?" Sam roared. "How dare you play with our lives for your own entertainment."

Trust me, young Guardian, no entertainment is ever garnered from these trials. They are designed for the sole purpose of allowing you to choose your own future.

"How could any of those experiences be considered a choice?" Sam spluttered.

The choice lay in your acceptance or denial of the reality of your situation. Your hearts and minds refused to accept what they did not understand, and rather than push the inconsistencies aside, you each pushed through the confusion and restored the memories. You chose to return to the place where your lives were in peril, rather than embrace the life you felt had been unfairly stripped away.

I swallowed down the bile rising up my throat. "And if we'd chosen the other way?"

You would have continued to live out your lives in that alternate reality, with no memory of what you'd both found and lost. You would not have been the first, nor would you be the last. Fate is a fickle mistress, and nothing is ever written in stone.

CHAPTER THIRTY-NINE

Sam

I was so over all this crap I wanted to punch something. I also wanted to get out of this damned cave and finally get to Zion. It would be such a relief to not have to deal with anyone or anything magical for a while. But I still needed to know more about something the voice had said. He'd called me a Guardian. *What the hell?* I was about to ask when the voice spoke again.

I am sorry you were forced to spend so much time in this place, but there is one more thing you need to understand before you enter Zion. Something I did not explain to our Little Saviour when we last spoke, was why the Guardians were so important to the world before the Magic Council took over. It is also the reason the Council hunts and disposes of Immunes as soon as one is exposed.

Okay, so it looked like I would get my explanation without having to ask my question. It was beginning to sound like being called a Guardian was an honour.

The Guardians of old were not just Immunes. They also wielded their own magic. The lie the Magic Councillors profess about Nothings being a throwback to a time before magic existed is one constructed by the Vizier responsible for the death of the Queen and her Guardians. You see, the Queen had the power to bestow and remove magic where she pleased. The Vizier was under investigation at the time for stirring up unrest, and if found guilty, the Queen would have removed his powers. And so... he killed them all before justice could be done.

"Whoa, whoa, whoa... I think you need to back up a bit. You don't seriously think I have this power the Queen had, right? Because I don't even have my own magic." Molly looked ready to cut and run any minute.

Aaahh, Little Saviour. You are indeed descended from the Queen's bloodline, and therefore possess her powers. At present, they are dormant within you, although I believe they may have emerged on a few occasions.

I thought about what Molly had done to the Councillor's car before we'd found them, and then what she'd done when we were under attack at the mine. She was something special all right. But hadn't I just been relishing getting away from magic in Zion? Did I really want to have my own?

"So... there've been no Guardians since they were all poisoned then?"

Oh yes, I knew there was something I had forgotten to tell you. As you step from the cave, you will be endowed with whatever is required to make you a Guardian. So, you and Tray will receive the gift of magic, and Sarah will acquire the gift of Immunity. As is the case with all those who reside in Zion.

Molly needs nothing as she already carries the power she will need inside her. Soon it will be time to wake what has been dormant for so long.

END OF BOOK 1

ABOUT THE AUTHOR

Thank you so much for reading *Nothing*. I hope you enjoyed reading it as much as I did writing it. I am currently writing book 2 and will have it finished and released as soon as humanly possible.

I'd love you to visit my website and sign up for my newsletter so you're kept in the know about further updates and release dates at:

jenniferredmile.com

P.S. I'd be forever grateful if you'd consider leaving a review on Amazon.